UNPAID DUES

Shelter was relieved when he finally removed the leg irons that had kept him in bondage for so long. Looking down at his ankles he could almost see bone through the bloody pulp.

When he looked up to see the beautiful Sylvia before him, he thought he was hallucinating and that he wasn't Zukor's prisoner. It had been months since he had seen—or touched—a woman. And as a hot, all-consuming passion rose up in his groin, she slowly undressed and exposed her firm, full breasts and luscious hips.

It was too much for him to resist. Within moments, their bodies were joined and rhythmically moving together.

Shell would soon pay for that pleasure, though. For in the distance, one of the guards had witnessed the act of love—between Shell and Zukor's niece. . . .

SPECTACULAR SERIES

NAZI INTERROGATOR (649, $2.95)
by Raymond F. Toliver
The terror, the fear, the brutal treatment, and mental torture of WWII prisoners are all revealed in this first-hand account of the Luftwaffe's master interrogator.

THE SGT. #3: BLOODY BUSH (647, $2.25)
by Gordon Davis
In this third exciting episode, Sgt. C.J. Mahoney is put to his deadliest test when he's assigned to bail out the First Battalion in Normandy's savage Battle of the Hedgerows.

SHELTER #3: CHAIN GANG KILL (658, $1.95)
by Paul Ledd
Shelter finds himself "wanted" by a member of the death battalion who double-crossed him seven years before *and* by a fiery wench. Bound by lust, Shelter aims to please; burning with vengeance, he seeks to kill!

GUNN #3: DEATH'S HEAD TRAIL (648, $1.95)
by Jory Sherman
When Gunn stops off in Bannack City he finds plenty of gold, girls, and a gunslingin' outlaw who wants it all. With his hands on his holster and his eyes on the sumptuous Angela Larkin, Gunn goes off hot—on his enemy's trail!

Available wherever paperbacks are sold, or order direct from the Publisher. Send cover price plus 50¢ per copy for mailing and handling to Zebra Books, 21 East 40th Street, New York, N.Y. 10016. DO NOT SEND CASH!

#3

SHELTER

CHAIN GANG KILL
BY PAUL LEDD

ZEBRA BOOKS

KENSINGTON PUBLISHING CORP.

ZEBRA BOOKS

are published by

KENSINGTON PUBLISHING CORP.
21 East 40th Street
New York, N.Y. 10016

Printed in the United States of America

1.

Shelter Morgan was a long-jointed man, but just now he was folded up and squeezed into an iron tub, soaking off the grime of weeks on the desert. With the coarse lye soap he scrubbed his blond hair, singing a song as he did so.

Outside the day was bright, cloudless for as far as the eye could see, and that took in most of Arizona on a day like this—or seemed to at least. A mocking bird perched on the open window, strutted back and forth, then cocked its head curiously at the sight of the tall man, lathered from head to foot crammed into that galvanized tank. Then it flew off, scolding the day or Shelter Morgan.

Shell laughed, dipped his face to the water and sat up, arms flopped out of the tub, toes curled up over the lip. "Did you get your back?"

Shell turned his head to Alicia who stood behind him, dressed only in a pale pink wrapper, her dark hair falling across her shoulders, down her back.

"Couldn't reach it," he smiled. "How 'bout a hand?"

Alicia dipped into the tub and took the sponge. Shell closed his eyes, enjoying the soothing circular scrubbing of his back. Then Alicia leaned forward, dipping the sponge into the water once again, and he felt the smooth softness of her bare breasts against his soapy back.

"Really gettin' into it, aren't you?"

"I will," she answered. She leaned forward once more, kissing his neck, taking a small, teasing bite.

"Never work," Shell answered. Alicia wrung out the sponge, letting the water trickle down his hard-muscled back. Then she stepped around in front of him, wearing nothing but a deep smile.

"It'll work," she promised.

Shell let his eyes caress Alicia's long legs, her full hips. Her breasts were magnificent, slightly uplifted, with prominent nipples. Just now they were damp with the soapy water as was the dark, soft triangle between her thighs.

Lithely she stepped in the tub, facing Shelter, and standing above him. Shell felt the excitement growing in him as she stood there, the heavy throb-

6

bing between his legs building. Alicia looked down, seeing the head of his erection bobbing above the soapy water and she smiled, slowly easing down.

Her buttocks slid down on Shell's upraised thighs and she managed to settle on his crotch, supporting herself with her hands on the side of the tub.

"Just don't capsize us," Shell said.

"I don't care right now," Alicia said. Slowly she began to wash Shell's chest, his shoulders, leaning far forward to kiss his mouth.

Shell had the sponge in his hand now and reaching out, he ran it down her back, across her shoulders, and those pendulous, tantalizing breasts which swayed before his hungry eyes.

Alicia put her hand on Shell's thighs and scooted back up a ways, her dark eyes closed. She sucked at her lower lip in expectation as her hand dipped into the water, finding Shell's shaft.

"Mm." She let her fingers search him slowly, and Shell could touch and see the slight quivering in her thigh muscles. Slowly she positioned herself, touching the head of the shaft to her silky, inner lips. "Now," she murmured and she settled slowly onto him, the warm water intensifying the sensation.

As she felt Shell touch bottom she leaned far forward, her hands running over his soapy, hard shoulders, and back; her mouth met his in a lusty kiss, her tongue going deep within his mouth as she slowly swayed, lifting her hips slightly then driving her pelvis against Shelter's.

Shell put a hand behind her head, holding that pliant, demanding mouth to his. He held her neck, a handful of her heavy black hair, devouring her with his own kisses as she rocked, ever faster, against him.

With his free hand Shell cupped her breasts, first one then the other, squeezing the taut nipples between his fingers. Then his hand ran down along her abdomen, along her firm, trembling thighs, and he felt the muscles jump beneath his palm.

Alicia threw her arms around Shell's neck, and Shell's hands dropped into the water, finding her buttocks which he squeezed hard, drawing her urgently to him. It was building in him now and in Alicia as well.

She threw her head back, eyes distant, mouth open with cadenced breathing. Shell's head went to her breasts, his mouth tasting the film of soap as he licked her breasts, suckling then biting lightly those firm, brown nipples.

Alicia slid up his thighs, her hands going into the water to find Shell, to feel all of him as she drove against him, her hips rising and falling as she buried Shell in her depths.

"I can't . . . no more," Alicia said in a distant voice. Then she quickened her pace, and her hips and thighs slapped against Shell under the water as he held to her buttocks, not wanting to lose her as she worked herself to a frenzy of need.

"Now, baby," he whispered. Her ear was next to his mouth, and he parted her hair, whispering again. "Now, baby."

Alicia worked now with a fierce concentration, Shell encouraging her with words, tiny touches. She panted in his ear, her tongue searching it, then again her lips, incredibly soft, full went to his mouth.

Shell kissed her deeply, feeling her go suddenly rigid, her fingers kneading his shoulders, her thighs locking him inside of her.

She sat up suddenly, head thrown back, breasts upthrust, eyes closed in concentration, then she sagged against him, her hips giving a series of small convulsive pushes. Then she came undone.

Shell could feel the muscles inside of her tense then relax utterly as tiny waves of release swept through her. Alicia felt Shell driving against her now, wanting to come, and she raised herself just slightly, enough so that he could arch himself, controlling the strokes. He moved slowly at first, bringing Alicia back up again and she held still, allowing him his own pace.

Then there was no more holding back. She crouched over him—damp, warm, naked—and his eyes, taking in her lush figure, as much as the hot sensation between his legs brought him to a pulsing, deep climax.

Shuddering Alicia settled against him as Shell, still wanting her, twitched inside of her. She kissed his throat, his chest, her hands clawing at his arms.

It was too much, cramped up like that and Shell drew her mouth to his for one more lingering kiss. Then he took her shoulders and bit at her smooth throat.

"Get to the damned bed," he told her. "Now!"

Alicia stood, shakily, and stepped from the tub. Shelter was to her in a second, splashing water across the floor of the hotel room. He scooped

Alicia up and strode across the room, placing her on her back in the center of the bed.

"You're an animal," Alicia taunted.

"I know."

Shell climbed into bed, pressing his body against hers in a lingering embrace, kissing her mouth, breasts, abdomen. Slick with the tub water he slid on top of her, his thighs sliding over hers.

His palm slid across her abdomen and found the damp, soft bush there. Alicia responded instantly as his fingers dipped into her cleft, finding it dewy, warm.

Her hand slid down and joined his momentarily, feeling her own juices on his strong fingers. Then she reached for his erection, giving a small groan of satisfaction as she found it.

She lifted her knees slowly, spreading herself to Shell's caressing fingers. "Don't make me wait — I can't," she whispered and he let her guiding fingers place him inside of her.

Slowly, methodically he drove into her, deeply. He rolled from side to side and Alicia, eyes closed, head back on the pillow, followed his motions with those of her own pelvis.

"So good," she murmured. "It is so very good the way you do it," she breathed. Then she gave a tiny, throttled scream and she pulled Shell's body to hers, kissing his face as he thrust more deeply yet into her soft depths, feeling her honey on their thighs.

"Don't wait." She threw her arms around him, clenching him with all of her strength and Shell's muscles tensed and he climaxed, sending an answering, shuddering tremor through Alicia. A tremor which began in her thighs and spread across her pelvis, running up to her tingling breasts until some deep well of emotion was opened to pour out her joy.

She swayed with Shell, slowly milking the last of this kindness from him. A tear ran across her cheek, staining the pillow beneath her long, raven black hair.

"My God!" she panted. "My God, Shelter."

They lay still for a long while, kissing each other, touching. Alicia ran her fingers across his hard chest, toying with the golden, curly hair there. She touched his shoulder, noticing the long jagged scar which ran across the knotted muscles there.

Shell lay his head against her breasts, letting her stroke his head, his back. He yawned and shut his eyes, only briefly he thought, yet when he opened them again hours had passed. Long shadows marked the hardwood floor of the hotel. A tint of coming sunset colored the pale skies outside.

Alicia slept too and Shell sat up in bed, drawing the sheet to his waist. There was a tap at the door and Shelter frowned. Alicia sat up instantly, drawing the sheet up over her breasts.

Shell's hand slid beneath the pillow and found the cold steel of his Colt revolver. He thrust the pistol under the sheets, his thumb on the hammer.

"Come in," he called.

The door opened and a hesitant face appeared. It was a girl dressed in trail clothes, carrying a long-barreled old rifle-musket. Not more than sixteen, it seemed, she had mouse brown hair and a face full of freckles. Just now, though, her face was mostly eyes as she gawked at Shelter Morgan and Alicia, and the girl's face flushed pink to the tips of her ears.

"I'm . . . I'm sorry," she stammered. "I was looking for a man."

"You sure found one, Honey," Alicia said with a smile which flushed the girl's face to crimson.

"A Mister Morgan," she said hurriedly.

"I'm Morgan," Shell said, "is it important?"

"It is, sir . . . my Grampa would like to speak with you . . ."

"All right. If you'll step out into the hall there, I'll get dressed."

"Yes, sir," she gulped. Again her eyes went to Alicia and she backed from the room. Alicia laughed and let her head fall back against the pilow.

"There was a time I could blush," she said, not with bitterness—it was simply a remembering. She watched as the tall blond man rolled from the bed and crossed the room.

Her eyes went to his heavily muscled thighs, the hard, concave buttocks. "God, you're a hell of a man, Shelter Morgan," she said under her breath.

Shell stepped into his jeans and pulled on his faded red shirt, finding two buttons missing. He frowned, stomped his feet into his boots and crossed to the mirror, seeing his own sharply featured face, the cool blue-gray eyes above his high cheekbones.

He dipped his face to the blue porcelain basin and rinsed off, dragging his fingers through his long, blond hair. Then he flipped his gunbelt on, retrieving the Colt from the bed.

"Don't be long," Alicia said.

He leaned across and kissed her, "No longer than I have to be."

Snatching up his dusty hat—which once had been white, but which the desert and time had shaded to a deep cream—he walked to the door, turning to wink once more at Alicia who smiled.

She was standing there waiting, when Shell came through the door and she was a little sprout. Shell was a tall man, and that had a lot to do with it, but she barely came up to the middle of his chest.

"Penny Dolittle," she said, sticking out a small hand which Shell took soberly. She had a tiny, turned-up nose and a no-nonsense manner. She held that old muzzle-loader as if she knew what it was for. Her coat was shabby, two sizes too big, and she wore faded jeans stuffed into worn boots.

"You say your grandfather wants to talk to me?" Shell asked.

"That he does," she nodded, "if you *are* Shelter Morgan."

"None other," Shell replied with a smile, but Miss Penny Dolittle did not respond to the smile.

"Then come along," she said, "this is a serious matter, and I had to be sure."

Shell suppressed another smile and only nodded seriously. The girl gave her head a brisk nod and turned away, waving a hand. "You come along with me, Mister Morgan. There's things that need straightening out."

Shelter followed her down into the dining room

which was crowded that time of the evening, with soldiers, cowboys and teamsters. Plates clattered and the sweet smell of apple pie drifted from the kitchen. Shell stopped.

"He's not here, sir," Penny said. "Outside. Grampa's out back in our wagon."

She marched right across that dining room with Shell striding after her. Eyes lifted from the tables and a few smiles followed the peppery young girl with a musket in her hand.

It was dark in the alley. The moon was rising late these nights and Shell waited a minute for his eyes to adjust to the darkness.

Penny Dolittle, who had been bounding ahead stopped, stared and tapped her toe impatiently. "What is it?" she asked.

"I'm comin'," Shell replied, shaking his head. She was all spice, this one, headstrong and pert. There was an old battered Conestoga wagon around the corner and Shell followed her toward it.

"Up the steps," she directed him, and Shell went ahead, ducking his head to clear the canvas and hoop. There was a candle, burned low near the front of the wagon interior. The smoke lifted to a small cutout in the canvas. Beside the candle, propped in a wooden chair, was an old timer with a face full of white whiskers.

"Morgan?" the old man asked, glancing up.

"That's right," Shell answered.

"Good." He nodded, smiling a little toothlessly. "Hold steady on him, Penny! You, Shelter Morgan, you can shuck that Colt you're wearing or get your belly blown open."

14

Shell heard the ominous cocking of the muzzle loader behind him, and he glanced across his shoulder. She must have had to use both thumbs to cock that old musket, but it was cocked, and primed.

"Just take it easy," Shell said softly. The old man was grinning like the cat with a canary.

"I mean to. Jest make damned sure you do! Penny, keep a light finger on that trigger. He's a dangerous one. Now! I told you to drop that Colt revolver, Morgan."

Slowly Shell unbuckled his gunbelt, flipping it to the old man. "All right?"

"Fine. Jest fine," the old-timer said. "Now, Mister Morgan . . . if you'd oblige me. Drop your pants!"

"What . . . are you touched, old-timer?"

"You heard me! Unbuckle that belt of yourn and drop your trousers, Morgan. Or take a seventy caliber musket ball in the back—it's your choice."

2.

Shelter Morgan stood there in that smoky old Conestoga wagon, facing the old man, the girl with that muzzle loader behind him, her finger on the trigger. Still he had not moved—had he heard that man right? He repeated it.

"Drop your trousers, Morgan. Do it now!"

Now that was something—there had now and then been an anxious woman who spoke to him in about the same way, but the girl behind him wasn't that sort. Besides, it was the old-timer with the fuzzy face who was doing the asking.

Shell obliged. He had been brought up not to argue with his elders . . . or a loaded gun.

The old man peered closely at him, then nodded with apparent satisfaction, spitting a stream of tobacco juice on the floor of the wagon.

"That does it—that scar, looks like a bullet wound to me."

Shell nodded. There was a nasty, star shaped scar in his right thigh. "It is."

"All right. Pull them trousers up, Morgan."

"Mind tellin' me what this is about?" he asked.

"Oh, I'll tell you. You can bet on that," Dolittle answered. He told Penny, "Keep that rifle on him, honey. I'll tie him up."

The old-timer was to him in three steps, cautiously moving behind him. Shell felt the bite of rawhide as the old man crossed his wrists behind him and tied his hands with a pair of tight figure eights.

"Now," Dolittle panted. "On your belly, Morgan."

"This has gone far enough," Shell said angrily.

"Poke him, honey."

The muzzle of that musket felt cold, deadly against Shell's spine. He doubted the girl would shoot. A little bit of female like that . . . or would she?

He got to his knees and then to his belly on the boards of the Conestoga and Dolittle hogtied him like a branding calf.

"I won't leave you like that, wouldn't be hoomane," Dolittle snorted. "It's jest till we clear town."

Shell started to object, but Dolittle shut him up with a warning. "You keep your mouth shet! Penny, give me that firearm, and you climb up in the box. We got our man, let's get rolling!"

Shell watched the girl step past him. He craned his neck, wanting to see Dolittle's face, but it was awkward, and he gave it up.

"There's people waiting for me," Shell told him. "When I don't come back . . ."

"I reckon she'll jest find herse'f another man if you don't come back, which you ain't," Dolittle sniffed. The old man was squatting against the tailgate, musket across his knees.

Shelter heard the girl release the brake and speak softly to the horses. The wagon lurched forward, then rolled on through the streets of Fort Bowie, the wheels squeaking on a dry hub.

There was a pause after ten minutes or so, the wagon halting at the gate, no doubt, and Shell considered giving a yell, but Dolittle must have been reading his mind.

"Don't you dare make a sound," he said, and Shell felt the cold nudge of that musket behind his ear. The wagon creaked on, turning right — northward — at the fork.

The Conestoga bounced and swayed. Shell's face was flat against the floor, and from time to time the planks slapped up at his jaw and chin as the wagon hit a chuckhole. He was getting damned mad now, but there was nothing to do about it. Dolittle chuckled to himself as Shelter muttered a slow, profuse curse.

The wagon jolted on for mile after mile, across the dark, empty desert. Shell lay bound, cramped

18

against the floor. They had been travelling for nearly three hours, by Shell's best estimate when the wagon finally shuddered to a stop.

He lifted his head expectantly, but Dolittle told him. "Don't get too excited, son. We only stopped to move you some. Cain't be too comfortable trussed up like that. Like I say, I am a hoo-mane soul. Wouldn't want you to suffer needlessly.

"I reckon you'll suffer plenty once we get to Strawberry."

"Strawberry? Where's that?"

"Navajo county, son. North a ways. Nice country, if I say so my ownself. We're from Strawberry, Penny and myself. Just outside, I should say— Grizzly Run, they call it."

Dolittle gave Shell enough of a hand so that he was able to get to his knees and finally to a sitting position against the wagon box, facing Dolittle who sat in the rear.

"Take it on ahead, Penny!" Dolittle shouted and again the Conestoga started rolling northward. Shell watched the old man, searched the wagon interior. There was nothing but a pile of old and aromatic hides, a flour barrel, the chair in which Dolittle sat, a locked trunk.

The rawhide ties were cutting off the blood to Shell's hands. He could feel the prickly beginning of numbness in them. Twisting his wrists, he felt for any give. There was none.

"Might as well set tight, Morgan. You'll not get free of one of Benjamin Dolittle's knots." He paused, spitting on the floor once again. "And if you did—well, I'd jest have to cut you in two with this musket, wouldn't I?"

"Why would you?" Shell asked. "You owe it to me to tell me what's happening here, don't you?"

"Don't know's how I *owe* you anything. But I'll tell you . . . just as if you didn't know."

Carefully the old man dipped a hand inside his coat pocket and brought out a yellowed piece of heavy paper. He unfolded it, squinting at it in the dim light of the candle.

"What's that?" Shelter wanted to know.

"What is it! Boy, it's your wanted poster." He turned the paper toward Shelter and he frowned, seeing his own name in inch-high block letters beneath the black "Wanted."

"For murder," Dolittle read. "Shelter Morgan. Six foot, three inches—you're a tall one, ain't you?" Dolittle peered at him, measuring, "You didn't look that tall to me . . . blond hair, gunshot wound on right thigh. Well," he shrugged putting the wanted poster away, "if that ain't you, it's your twin with the same name."

"I never been in Navajo county," Shell said.

"No? Must've been mighty near to it. A man died, there's folks said you did it."

"A man? What was his name?" Shelter asked.

"Lewis Hart."

"Never heard of him."

"No?" Dolittle shrugged again. "Mebbe he didn't have time to tell you his name."

"I'm telling you I didn't kill anyone," Shell said in exasperation. "There's some sort of mistake."

"Could be, I reckon," Dolittle nodded. "You tell it to Sheriff Chambers."

Chambers. True, it was not an uncommon

name, but it was possible. "Wesley Chambers?"

"That's right," Dolittle said, squinting at Shell. "You know *him*, do you?"

"Wes Chambers. Yeah, I know him," Shell answered. From long back, from Georgia.

They rode silently, immersed in their own thoughts for the time being. Dolittle seemed nearly ready to nod off, his whiskers resting on his chest, and Shell thought of having a try for that gun, hogtied or not. It beat hanging all to hell.

"Don't try it," Dolittle yawned. "I'd have to kill you, boy. I'd rather the law did that."

"Mind telling me how you found me?" Shell asked.

"Nothin' to it." Dolittle took off his battered flop hat and scratched his white-fuzzed head. "Got a friend named Roy Greif—he's a teamster, running army freight. Come a week ago, maybe ten days, he pulled into Strawberry. Roy, he happened to have a newspaper from Bowie with him. He al'ays gives 'em to me. There ain't much to read around, and it's good for the girl to practice her readin'.

"Come to read about a big to-do down this way. A wagon train of Quakers massacred, and only one survivor. A man named Shelter Morgan, it said. You reported that Apache attack."

"I see."

"So I pondered on that name. Shelter Morgan. Danged if it don't come to me, out of the blue. I seen that poster hanging in the sheriff's office for nearly a year. Yes, sir . . ."

"You some kind of amateur bounty hunter?" Shell asked sourly.

"No, sir," Dolittle wagged his head, "never have been. But this year, she's been a hard one. I only got me and the girl. Got a little dirt farm. Few cows . . . you know how it is. But it didn't rain, and things baked up. Banker, he knows better than to lend me money I'll never be able to pay back. So I thought hard about you. Real hard, and then we tried it. Amateur—I reckon," he smiled, "but mister, we got you."

The wagon had stopped again. They had been travelling up a grade for a long while. Now, apparently they had reached the crest.

"We'll get down for a while," Dolittle said. "Have some coffee and beans."

"It'll be kind of hard for me," Shell muttered.

Penny poked her head in from the box, her nose twitching as she studied Shelter Morgan. "We're at Big Crest, Grampa."

"Good. Give me a hand, Penny."

The girl took the rifle as Dolittle untied Shell's hands, leaving his ankles bound. Then he retied the knots, in front. "Think you can hobble down?" he asked.

"I'll try it," Shell answered. Slowly he got to his feet and hopped toward the tailgate, the girl following him with the musket. Turning around he managed to slide to the ground.

It was still, star bright. A half moon hung near the horizon. There were a pair of huge old oaks just off the road, and Ben Dolittle nodded toward them. Hopping all the way, Shell made the big trees and with a heavy sigh he sagged against the trunk of one, settling to the ground.

"Jest fine," Dolittle nodded his pleasure. He had the musket again, and he sat across from Shell on a fallen limb, stoking a small fire. Penny was walking from the wagon, packing a coffee pot, some cans and a fire-blackened pot.

"He confess to his wrong-doin' yet, Grampa?" she asked, glaring at Shell.

"Not yet. Says he's innocent."

"Well, sure, and don't they all. Him!" she huffed. "Why I knew the moment I saw him!"

Shell only grinned at the little pepper-pot and that seemed to infuriate her. She slammed the pot to the ground and began working on one of the cans with her knife.

"Don't cut a finger," Shell said mildly, as if speaking to a child.

"I won't, don't you worry!"

And if she had cut one off right then she wouldn't have let Shell know. He leaned back against the tree, making himself as comfortable as possible. Penny dumped the beans into the pot, the juice hissing against the fire.

"Hope there ain't no Apaches around," Shell said idly, looking around the dark hillsides.

"There ain't no Apaches," Penny said confidently, her hands on her hips as she faced Shelter across the fire. "That Thumb and his renegades are down into Mexico now, fighting the Mexican army. The paper said that too!"

"He *was* there," Shell agreed. "But you know them Apaches. They could be most anywhere."

"You don't scare me, Mister Morgan."

Nevertheless, Shell noticed the girl's eyes going to

the shadows from time to time and he grinned at Dolittle. The old man frowned in return, shaking his head.

He handed Shell a cup of coffee, scalding hot, strong as stink, and he sipped at it, watching them eat. Penny hunkered over her plate, shoveling it in. She must have felt Shelter's eyes on her for she looked up suddenly.

"Something the matter?"

"No."

"Changed your mind, want some beans?"

"No thanks."

"Well you were looking at something!" she snapped.

"I just don't see many moles," Shell said to her. She cocked her head, not understanding.

"I can see well enough, Mister Morgan."

"That's not what I meant."

"Then what did you mean?"

"Nothin'. It's only that a mole, he can't go no more than eight, nine hours without eating or he starves to death."

Penny put her fork on her tin plate. Her mouth opened, started to say something, then shut. The red light of the fire hid the hot flush which crept up into her face. Her eyes seemed to have caught some of that fire, the way they sparked at Shelter Morgan.

"You sure got a way of charmin' the girls," Dolittle said. The old man shook his head, picking up his own coffee.

"*Some* ladies find him charming, Grampa. Certain kinds of ladies. I reckon they appreciate his low form of humor."

24

Shell answered in a low voice, "I reckon I find them a little more charming too. I never was hogtied and kidnapped by any woman I met, until now."

Penny said nothing in return. Her eyes seemed to soften for a moment. Then she turned her face back to her plate. But she put it aside without eating more.

They sat silently for a time after that, the old man stoking up a corncob pipe, Shell drinking his second cup of coffee with his bound hands.

The embers were burning low when Dolittle spoke again, his face merely a shadow across the fire ring. "You say you didn't do the killing. Is that true?"

"It's God's truth," Shell answered.

"But can you prove it, boy?"

"Does it matter?"

"To me, it does. I think I'm doing the right thing. By the girl, by the law. Taking you back, I mean. But I'd hate to think I was putting the noose around an innocent man's neck."

"That's just what you're doing," Shelter told him.

"But you can't prove it."

"Prove it! All I can tell you is what I said before. I never been through Strawberry, never met a man named Lewis Hart. Never murdered anybody."

"How'd your name come to be on the poster," Dolittle wanted to know, "that bein' the case?"

"It's a long story," Shell shrugged. "Your county sheriff, I know him from a long ways back. I figure he's fishin' for me, hopin' somebody would see that poster and bring me in."

"Like I'm doin'," Dolittle commented.

"That's right."

"I'd not like to think that's true," Dolittle said sincerely. "Why don't you give me your story, boy? It don't cost me none to listen."

"All right," Shell answered. "I can tell you about it."

"Then do it," Dolittle replied striking a match which he touched to his dead pipe, "and tell it all to me—straight. 'Cause if you don't, son, I'm most afraid you're going to hang."

3.

It had grown cooler. A frosty ring circled the high moon, and the stars seemed near, cold. Dolittle shook the coffee pot, offered the last of it to Shell and put a few small sticks on the embers, prodding the fire to life.

The flames twisted and sparked, casting flickering shadows across the faces of Dolittle and Penny. She was silent now, hands wrapped around her knees as she stared into the fire.

Shell took a swallow of the coffee and with a

deep breath he began at the beginning, deep in Georgia, the war at its bloody tag-end.

"We were camped down along the Conasauga River. We hadn't seen a thing but the fire from the Federal cannon, the blood of our own in months. At night the flames swept across Georgia, lighting it as bright as day. Sherman was on the march, putting the torch to our last hopes. We were shoeless, thirsty, exhausted. Yet we fought on—why, I can't say. When men start up fightin', sometimes they just keep on, even when there's no longer any sense to it.

"At night the yells of the wounded kept us awake, the food was gone. Everything but hope was gone, burned away or shelled to hell . . ."

"It must have been terrible," Penny put in. Shelter nodded in reply.

"More terrible, Miss, than anything you could imagine if you tried. Men lay strewn everywhere. There was little time for the buryin'. Very bad . . . that was where I met this Wes Chambers. Down along the Conasauga. We were both in Colonel Fainer's command."

Shell closed his eyes. Even now he could see it when he did that. See the streaming sulphurous flares overhead, hear the bombardments which followed, feel his heart racing.

"Morgan? Captain Morgan?"

Shelter Morgan's eyes flickered open. Squinting into the fierce sunlight he was able to make out the haggard features of Corporal Chambers. Wide shouldered, narrow waisted, the man had oily, brown eyes and a chin which turned out.

"What's up?"

"Colonel Fainer wants to see you, sir," Chambers told him.

"Now?"

"Now sir."

Shell stretched his arms, yawning heavily. His eyes were red-rimmed, and when he blinked it felt like ground glass beneath his eyelids.

Shelter Morgan straightened his tunic and dusted off, following the corporal through the camp. He stepped down painfully on a stone and he grimaced. Well, he had started out barefoot in this army, and it looked like he would end up the same way. There was a dollar-sized hole in that boot.

He had come up out of Tennessee, reporting with a grin and a squirrel gun that went back two generations. The war had seemed adventurous then, and by sticking his neck out farther than some others, Shell had been rewarded with field promotions.

It had been a long road through this war. Moving forward, and later doing a lot of backing up.

Shell had worn the gray for four years now, most of them being lean, bitter years. He had served under Beauregard at bloody Manassas, and later at Front Royal and Cross Keys under Jackson. That was the first time he had been wounded, and it was there he was promoted to captain.

For the last year it had been a series of nameless, dirty skirmishes, a rolling back to defensive positions, then rolling back farther as their ranks dwindled, the ammunition grew scarce.

There was nothing left of that thrill of battle, the desire for glory, only a cold determination to survive this blood letting.

Shelter was waved on through into Colonel Fainer's tent, and he lifted the flap, slipping inside. Fainer sat at the head of a table — if such it could be called, his dark eyes searching Shelter Morgan as he came in from the brilliant sunlight.

"Captain Morgan."

"Colonel." Shell saluted, noticing the assembly of officers in the tent. They stood along the tent wall or sat in chairs at the table.

Major Twyner was there, sour as ever. The Georgian had lost an arm and replaced it with bitterness. Captain Bowlen who was a hoarder stood beside Twyner.

Leland Mason scowled in response to Shell's glance. The Mississippian was an aristocrat with a plantation back home . . . or so he still hoped.

"Make yourself comfortable, Shelter. Sit down," Fainer said.

Shell nodded and dragged up a barrel to perch on. It was only then that he saw the officer standing in the corner of the tent, immersed in shadows.

The man took a step forward and a patch of sunlight illuminated the insignia of a general officer.

"Captain Morgan, this is General Custis."

"Sir."

"Don't get up, Captain," the general said, waving a hand. "If you don't mind, Colonel Fainer?" The colonel shrugged, lighting a cigar, and Custis went on, "I understand you know Tennessee, Captain Morgan."

"Know it? It's home. Lived my boyhood up near Pikeville."

"Isn't that near Chickamauga, Captain?"

"It is. Right near."

"Chickamauga was a bitter defeat, Captain." The general was silent, eyes turned down for a moment. He lifted them again to Shell. "It was a turning point. The losses were incredibly heavy."

The general was again silent. Nobody stirred in the tent. A single fly droned across the room. Abruptly the general turned back sharply toward Shell.

"Can you get through to Chickamauga, Morgan?"

"The general can't be serious." Shell was grinning, but the grin faded from his lips as Custis's green eyes revealed that he was not kidding in the least.

"Sir, Sherman's got us surrounded. Bragg and Hood together couldn't break out of Georgia just now."

"I'm not speaking of General Bragg or of Hood, Captain. I'm speaking about you. Can you get to Chickamauga?"

"I might . . ." Shell glanced at Colonel Fainer who nodded.

"With a company of men?" Custis wanted to know. He was nearer to Shell now, his eyes piercing.

"No, sir," Shell had to tell him. "Not with a company."

"Then with a handful of men . . . in civilian clothes?"

"Sir," Morgan said softly, sincerely, "I swore I wouldn't take off the gray until this war was done."

"It is done, damnit!" Colonel Fainer shouted, slamming his palm against the table.

"And lost," Custis added flatly, "unless we can procure vast, immediate assistance. And *that* is why it is essential that you get through to Chickamauga, if there is the slightest chance. The slightest opportunity for success."

Shell was silent, thoughtful for a long moment. He sat with his arms crossed, looking to the other officers in the tent. Fainer watched back expectantly, Mason fidgeted in his chair.

General Custis stood there woodenly, and Shell studied the man. He had the bearing of an aristocrat, but that rigidity had been shaped some by the war. He spoke the men's jargon now, reacted less strongly to breaches of the code. A man nearing fifty, with silver hair curled up over his collar, he was intent, anxious, and it showed.

Shell answered slowly. "Supposing I could take the high ridges and break through into Tennessee. Supposing I had a handful of men with me—two, three, no more. What in hell could we accomplish?"

"A stay of execution," Custis replied caustically. "Time—some time, perhaps enough to mount a counter-offensive. Even now if we could convince the Federals that we still have teeth, the nerve to use them, we could win some softer terms at inevitable surrender, Morgan."

"And food," Fainer interrupted, "clothing against a hard winter. Medicine for our wounded and ill—that is what could be gained by such a venture, Captain."

"Ammunition," Major Twyner put in angrily. Since losing that arm at Malvern Hill he had become utterly savage, vindictive.

"I don't see how . . ." Morgan began, but Custis cut him off impatiently.

"*Can* it be done, Captain?"

Shell hesitated. "It wouldn't be easy."

"I recognize that, Captain! The question is—can it be done?"

"I reckon so. With luck." Morgan took a deep breath. "You lay it out for me. Tell me what you expect, and I'll give it what I've got, sir."

It was a suicide mission, no one had to explain that. Yet there was a chance, as Custis said, that the laying down of arms while on the offensive might help soften the surrender terms. None of them had any idea that the Union terms would be less than brutal, reducing the South to poverty if an unconditional surrender had to be signed. If an offensive might help alleviate some of the suffering, leaving the people with something of dignity, it would be worth it.

It was of the wounded, too, Shell thought. There had been moments when Shell would have traded any possession for an ounce of morphine to beat back the pain from a gangrenous leg, a shot-away skull. Friends lay dying, screaming from a pain which would not abate. And more soldiers of the Confederacy were dying of the cold than from

Union bullets just now. There were simply no blankets, no boots.

If anything could be done to alleviate any of this . . . yet Shell was puzzled. How was any of it possible under present circumstances?

Custis explained it. "When Sherman pushed General Bragg out of Chickamauga, we left much behind." He stroked his silver mustache, watching Shell's eyes. "I was there, and I know. Mules were left behind, cannon, Confederate boys. Medical supplies."

"All gone now," Morgan said quietly.

"All gone," Custis agreed. "The boys to prison camps, the medicine to the Union hospital camps, the mules used to draw our own cannon against us."

"But then . . .?"

"That wasn't all, Morgan. We left something else behind. At Lookout Mountain."

Shell raised a curious eyebrow and Custis waited a moment before coming out with it. The general glanced at Fainer and then said, "There was gold, Morgan. A lot of gold. My estimate is that it is nearly a quarter of a million dollars worth."

Shell whistled. A quarter of a million . . .

"It was army pay, money for provisions being shipped through to Lee in Virginia," General Custis explained. "Yet there was no way through to Virginia, and the couriers were forced to take refuge with Bragg at Chickamauga.

"Then, as you know, Sherman broke our backs and we withdrew. Helter-skelter. They tore us apart at Lookout, and our counter-offensive was repulsed. We retreated to Georgia hurriedly, sir. Without the gold."

"It is still at Lookout?"

"It is, sir. Buried deeply. I can show you the exact location, and I will if you will attempt retrieving it."

"You may pick your own men, set your own timetable," Fainer put in. "Use whatever routes and methods you choose. But retrieve that gold, Shell, everything depends on it."

Shelter Morgan strode back to his own tent, turning the thing every which way in his mind. He tried to make vivid his memories of Lookout Mountain, of Chickamauga, the Great Smoky Mountains—all places he remembered with fondness from a simpler time.

He had walked the high ridges, a barefoot boy with an eye for squirrels, a creek to drop a line into, never seeing it as a potential battlefield, a place where men came to die.

There was a good bass hole near Lookout itself, if it hadn't been shelled, buried or filled with dead things . . . the bass had been nearly civilized there, along the Wind Fork, and a bit of bacon rind would net dinner. At times they would strike a bare hook, rising to break water, flashing silver in the bright morning sunshine before disappearing, rings of moving silver ripples marking the spot. Shell had once taken a six point buck in the Smoky Mountains without rising from his bed . . . it was a grand, majestic sweep of country, with the blue haze drifting among the scarlet and gold as the autumn trees turned.

All gone to warfire and cannon smoke. There was no time for remembering how it had once been, but only for grappling with the problem at hand.

It would take good men, tough and resourceful soldiers. Shell had four in mind. If they traveled the high ridges where no army could march, moving through the valleys by night, with luck they might make Tennessee. After that, it would be sheer luck, and Shell had never liked trusting to luck to do his work.

Shelter glanced up. His wrists were raw from the ties. Dolittle was still looking at him across the low fire. An owl called, away off down the long, dark hillsides.

"What happened?" the old man wanted to know.

"We made it," Shell said, and there was still some pride in saying that. "I picked a good crew. Thornton, he was rough as a bull, a good sergeant. Welton Williams—he was quick on the shoot, there was said to be trouble in his background, gun trouble.

"Little Dink wore spectacles. Mild, he was, but like an Indian in the wild. He could forage a meal off bare rock, it seemed. Keane—he lifted up at the wrong time and a Union sniper picked him off. We left Keane in Tennessee."

"But you made it back, the rest of you? With all that gold?"

"We did," Shell assured Dolittle. "It was hairy, believe me, but come through we did. Through Union lines each way."

"Seems like a man would've thought of not goin' back," Dolittle said thoughtfully. He chewed on his pipestem, watching Shell.

"It was a thought. Welton Williams, he brought it out in the open. To his way of thinking it was money destined to be wasted. There was no way we could win; every man-jack of us knew the war was lost. Why throw that money down the pipes?"

"But you didn't try it."

"No. I was a soldier, Dolittle. There were injured men, shoeless men depending on me. Williams was just frustrated with the waste—all of it. We came on back to Georgia."

"This doesn't seem to have much to do with Wes Chambers," Penny complained sleepily.

"It has a lot to do with him," Shell contradicted. "Only it wasn't just yet. We came back into Georgia, as I said, and moving through the broken country, carefully, we looked for Fainer's new position, knowing he had likely moved by then."

"You found him?"

"We found him. We followed a scout named Wakefield into a clearing and there we met them. All of them: officers, men in civilian clothes, their guns levelled on us. Welton Williams, he went down in a blaze of glory, both guns blasting until he had emptied them and they cut him to dog meat.

"Jeb, he was wounded and couldn't do much. They executed him. Me and the Dink were shot up, and we made our run . . . Dink didn't make it to sunset. Custis, Fainer, Plum . . . I have a list, Dolittle. Some of those names are crossed off now. I figure maybe Wes Chambers has gotten wind of that. He's on that list. He was there, and he helped murder my men."

Penny Dolittle was unimpressed, "That's a very nice story," she said, "yet there's no proof that a word of it is true, is there?"

"No, there's no proof. The witnesses are all dead," Shell replied grimly.

"And gold!" she continued, "Why, if Wes Chambers has a fortune stashed away, he doesn't live like it. Why would he be working for fifty a month as our sheriff?"

"I couldn't say," Shell said, lifting his cool blue eyes to the girl. "Chambers would have been low man on the totem pole. Probably his cut would have been small. Maybe he blew it all on one big fling. Maybe they cut him out completely. After all, he contributed nothing—aside from the fact he could put a real nice shine on the colonel's boots, as I recall."

"I'm more interested in another thing you said," Ben Dolittle said, rising stiffly from the cold fire. "You said you had made a list of the men who were there, those who massacred your soldiers. You also said," Ben peered at him from out of the shadows of the oak, "that some of those names had been crossed off."

"Four names," Shell replied.

"What does that mean exactly? Crossed off."

"They're dead," Shell was forced to admit, although he knew it wouldn't sound right.

"By your hand? Four men murdered?"

"Three of them. The Apaches got another."

"Reason I asked was . . . you sure you didn't have no Lewis Hart on that list?"

"I told you . . . !"

"I know it," Dolittle said calmly. "But it's strange a man admits to three murders and denies a fourth, naming the sheriff a liar."

"I know how it sounds. But those three men weren't cut down cold. They all had their chance to toss in their chips and live."

"Funny, ain't it," Dolittle said, "none of 'em did."

The old man kicked dirt over the embers of the fire, then he shook his head. "Sorry, son, I ain't convinced of a thing. I reckon the courts'll have to decide right and wrong."

"With Chambers county sheriff—you think I'll ever see a courtroom?" Shell asked bitterly. There was no reply to be made to that. They faced each other under the dark, star-spattered sky for a long, silent moment. Then Dolittle again helped Shelter to his feet, and he was placed in the wagon rolling toward Strawberry, a death warrant riding with him.

4.

Northward they rolled across the raw, empty land. Deserts of amber sand washed toward towering red buttes and wind-cut, stark spires. A series of low, fluted mesas lined out toward the horizon like a fleet of desert ships. The land was barren, painted in weird hues. Pinks and pale purples dominated the low areas, the yellow sands sun-bright in contrast.

Above them now, and to the east lay the broken remnants of a forest aged beyond time. Trees, once mighty and green lay petrified like the stony bones of some vanished mammoth creature. The wood had turned to jasper and agate, and it lay jumbled beneath the sand, with only a protruding trunk here and there to mark what had once been forest.

Nothing green grew here, or beyond where the salt-laden depressions marked a vanished sea. Only the tops of the mesas and the shallow washes were touched with the signs of life. A dull grayish green dotted these areas, showing the existence of sage or greasewood, with a sterile looking, thorny mesquite here and there.

The wagon lurched forward over rough, rain scoured roads which could hardly be called that. The day was hot; the wheel which was riding a dry hub produced a constant, nerve-grating squeal.

Shelter's hands were bound behind him, and they were bloodless, without sensation. His legs were cramped and his throat was dry. The wagon bounced over a rock and Shell swore deeply, imaginatively.

"Ought not to swear in front of the girl," Ben said, nodding toward the box.

"She ought to watch where she's driving this pile of firewood," Shell said shortly. Whatever patience he had had at the start of this trip had been worn to the nub. His nerves had raw endings, his scowl constant. "Can't you grease that damned hub!"

"Could," Ben nodded, spitting on the floor, "if'n I had some axle grease. But I ain't."

The air was close inside. Dolittle refused to open the canvas in the back for some reason known only to him. They swayed on, the silence deep and bitter between them.

"It won't be much longer," Dolittle said finally, and there was a touch of sympathy in his words. "Then at least you'll get untied."

"They'll tie me again," Shell answered. "One knot — around the neck."

Dinner was the same as breakfast had been, beans and sourdough. Shell ate his silently, refusing a cup of coffee. Once or twice Dolittle began to say something, but he always shut his mouth and turned away before he began. Shelter could see the man was suffering some, wrestling with his decision — but that just wasn't good enough.

Dolittle would go on feeling bad about it until they tripped the gallows and Shell swung dead. Then, with a handful of reward money he would quit feeling badly soon enough.

Dolittle took over the driving for a time, leaving Penny to guard Shelter. The girl was uncommunicative, and Shell felt no need to say anything. Only occasionally did their eyes meet, and the expression in her eyes looked as if he had slapped her. Quickly she turned her eyes down, cradling the musket in her arms.

They dipped low into a ravine and pulled a long grade, the horses straining. Dolittle had to use the whip to get the most from them. Cresting the grade they dropped a wheel into a rut, hard. Shell was thrown from his perch and the right side of the wagon tilted down crazily. When Dolittle tried to urge the team forward, there was a screeching from the bad wheel, and then a cracking shiver as the wheel broke free from the axle.

"Grampa!" Penny shouted.

"Wheel busted," he said with disgust. Shell heard the old man slip from the box and walk to the rear of the wagon. "Penny! I need some help."

"Morgan . . ." she said, her worried eyes going to Shell.

"Bring him out too!"

"All right, Mister Morgan. You heard Grampa. Take it easy now, move slow."

"I can't move any other way," Shell said angrily. He got to his feet and hopped along the tilted wagon bed, slipping out to the ground, Penny with her musket behind him.

Ben Dolittle had a tree limb and a rock, making a lever and fulcrum to raise that wagon. The wheel lay shattered, twisted beneath the axletree.

"Better let me help," Shelter said.

"The hell! Hold the musket steady on him, Penny!"

"Sit down, Mister Morgan," Penny said. Morgan sighed and did so. The girl covered him with that musket, her eyes flickering to where her grandfather worked futilely. The old man was breathing hard, perspiring. The sun was hot, the day clear. A horse blew and stamped its feet impatiently.

"I'm going to need your help, Penny," Dolittle said. "Come over here."

She walked to where Dolittle was, at the end of the lever, holding it down to elevate the wagon's back end.

"Put that musket beside you," the old man told her. "If he moves, shoot him."

"She's not heavy enough to hold that load, Dolittle," Shelter said. "Better let me lend a hand."

"No. No, sir," he said shaking his head decisively, "I want no stunts out of you. Not when we're this close to Strawberry."

"But, Grampa, if we left him tied . . ."

"No! No, Penny. Cain't you see those wheels spinning in his head. He's doin' what any man a prisoner does—tryin' to find some way out, any chance to make a break. No! I won't have him helpin'. Now then," Dolittle mopped at his forehead, frowning.

"If you can jest hold it up long enough fer me to prop it with some rocks . . . bring it level. Then we'll see about the wheel."

"All right, Grampa."

"And keep that musket near!" he shouted.

The girl frowned in response. Ben Dolittle was sometimes gruff, but there was no need for it just now. He was feeling a strain. Perhaps from holding the prisoner, perhaps from the sun. He was working harder than a man his age should be beneath such a fierce sun. It was well over a hundred degrees, with no trace of a breeze. The dust swirled up with every movement, filling the nostrils. Penny positioned herself at the end of the lever.

Dolittle was around the other side of the wagon, scrounging rocks to prop the axle up with. In a low voice, Shell told the girl, "It won't work, Penny. Let me help you. I can manage that lever even tied up."

"You heard Grampa," she replied, but she looked uncertain.

44

Dolittle had returned and he got to the dirt beside the wagon with a deal of effort. His face was utterly pale now. "Lean on that lever, Penny!" he called, and the girl did so, bringing the right rear up slowly.

"Now . . . hold it . . ." He managed to jam one large rock in under the axle, but Penny's grip loosened and he had to pull back quickly. "I told you to hold it!" he snapped.

"I'm doin' the best I can, Grampa. I can put the rocks under, if you'll pry."

"No. Now raise it again. Just raise it!"

Penny put her weight to it and the wagon creaked up another foot or so. Ben Dolittle shoved rocks in, forming a pyramid.

"Now, if you'll give it a hair more, Penny, a hair . . ."

"Grampa! I can't hold it!"

"Hold it, damnit!"

He slid beneath the axle, and Shell's muscles tensed. There was evident strain painted on the girl's face. The old man fumbled with a stone the size of his head, saw it roll away, and scooted farther under, groping for it.

"Grampa!"

Then it came down, the pyramid collapsing as Penny's hands slipped from the lever. Ben Dolittle screamed with pain as the axle crushed his chest, pinning him to the earth.

"Grampa!" Penny did nothing. She stood with her hands to her temples, eyes wide. Shell snapped her out of it.

"Damnit, untie me, Penny!"

"I . . ." she looked at him in confusion.

"Don't turn him loose!" Dolittle screamed. There was pain mingled with despair in his voice. Blood trickled from his nose and mouth.

"Penny. He'll die," Shell said softly and the girl nodded.

"No . . ."

Penny rushed to Shell, cutting him free with her pocket knife. Shell got to his feet, moving to the wagon, rubbing his wrists. He directed Penny, "Get back on that lever. Give it all you've got."

"I can't," she objected, eyes pleading, pained.

"You can! You did it once." He took her roughly by the shoulders, shaking her from her trance. "Do it again. Four inches. Raise it four inches and I'll drag him free. But move!"

Dolittle's mouth was open wide, painted crimson with the blood. His eyes watched as Shell crouched down and took a look.

"Tricked her. You tricked her, damn you!" He coughed, choking on the blood.

Shell glanced around at Penny who was ready at the lever. Reaching down he took Dolittle's ankles firmly. Then he nodded and Penny gave it all she had. The wagon rocked, lifted just slightly and Shell pulled, dragging Dolittle clear before the wagon collapsed again, crashing to the road, spewing yellow dust.

Shell picked Dolittle up and carried him in his arms to a patch of level ground out of the sun. Dolittle began coughing again, a terrible racking cough which told Shell his injuries were serious.

Penny rushed over to where her grandfather lay.

She carried the musket in her hand still, loosely; and as she raced past, Shell wrenched it from her hand. She seemed hardly to notice, but Dolittle did, and his eyes were accusing, hard.

"Gonna finish me, are you?" he panted.

Shell ignored the remark and kneeled beside Dolittle, opening his shirt to see what could be done. It was little enough. The skin was bruised horribly, and there was an indentation showing in the rib line.

"How is it?" Ben asked apprehensively.

"About the way you figure, I guess," Shell said, rocking back on his heels. "You need a doctor, and a good one. Fast."

"There's one at Holbrook," Penny said, lifting anxious eyes to the rough country to the west.

"How far?" Shell asked.

"Don't bother," Dolittle said, his words muted. He broke again into a terrible, blood choked cough. Now a bit of froth came up with his coughing—a lung had been punctured. "I'll not make it," the old man added.

"We can try!" Penny said.

"No." He put a hand on his granddaughter's wrist. He shook his head slowly. "I'd never make it, Penny. I know. I only regret that I'll be leavin' you sadly fixed. If you hadn't cut Morgan loose . . ." his head rolled toward Shelter, studying those cool, blue-gray eyes, the lean face of the blond man. "You was to be my legacy, Morgan. I got nothin' else to give the girl. Her folks, they died in a ranch fire. I wanted her to have an education," he coughed again and Shelter tried to quiet him, but

47

the old man shook his head vigorously.

"No! I never was one for bein' silent—even when it would have paid. Al'ays bull-headed, me. Stubborn, and now you see where my stubborness got me.

"I'm sorry, Penny," he said so low that Shell could hardly hear him. The girl took his hand, sitting, watching the breath slowly go out of Ben Dolittle.

Shell got to his feet, stretching his cramped legs, rubbing his wrists. He walked to the far side of the wagon and waited, watching sundown on the desert. A flight of dove winged low across the purpling sky. Somewhere a quail called and another answered from the underbrush.

"He's gone."

Penny was at Shell's elbow and he turned, his eyes going to the girl, then to the still figure of old Ben Dolittle beyond. "We'll bury him and put up a marker."

They scratched a hole with shattered spokes from the wagon wheel, scooping the earth from the grave with their hands. Finally Shelter stacked rocks on top of the grave, to prevent the coyotes from digging Ben up and scattering his bones. He stood with his hat off, watching the long sky fade to deep purple, a last scarlet thrust of the dying sun against a sheer cloud. Penny said no words out loud, but she stood, hat in hands, staring at the grave for a long while. It was nearly dark when she turned away, a tear streaking her dusty cheek.

"That's all there is to do, I reckon."

"I reckon."

"You." She turned to face Shell in the deep twilight. "What'll you be doing? Making your run, I expect."

Shell smiled thinly. He told her, "I'm going on toward Strawberry."

"Strawberry! Knowing what you do now?"

"Yes. Knowing what I do now," he said. Shell wiped back his hair and planted his hat. "Now I know that Wes Chambers is there. And he's a man I've been wanting to look up."

"He's the *law*," Penny objected.

"I know it."

She stared at the tall man, not comprehending. "He'll kill you."

"If I let him," Shell had to agree. "But I don't intend to. I want Wes Chambers as much, maybe more than he ever wanted me, Penny. I mean to have him."

"To kill him, you mean!" she said with obvious disgust.

"If he forces it. I'm not going there to assassinate him, Penny. But I couldn't muster up any sorrow for the man if it comes to having to do it."

She was silent a time, then she spoke, "Of course you'll have to kill him. How else can you get even? And that's what all of this is about, isn't it? Getting even. Your pride, your stubbornness—like Grampa's. . . ."

"It's not about getting even," Shell said quietly. He sat down on a rock at the edge of the road. "It's about three men these folks murdered. There should be the kind of law in this land which could track all of them down, try them and see to justice.

But there isn't. Men make their own laws out here, and you know it, Penny."

"You could have tried the Federal marshals."

"I spoke with some men in Washington once, long ago. They told me they figured there was no chance of findin' them, less of convicting them. Without evidence, witnesses."

"There was your testimony," she pointed out.

"Mine against that of twenty men. No—I don't want to kill any of them. It's just worked out that way. Funny thing is with some of them the gold was only channeled into other illegal activities. Like most thieves they get greedy and want more. Two of the men I shot would have been hung for later crimes if they had let me take them alive."

"You didn't bring that up before," Penny said.

"You didn't seem to have an abiding interest in my side of this, Penny. No—I didn't bring it up. Nor did I bring up the hundreds of other nameless men these murderers killed that day back in Georgia. Men who froze that winter, starved or died from lack of medicine that gold was supposed to buy. I knew them too, a part of them. I cared about 'em. My men. Not Chambers and those with him—he cared only about the gold, and likely, as you guess, it's all gone by now."

"Maybe . . . I didn't understand, I didn't really think about it like that," the girl said.

"No. I know it," Shell answered. After a while he asked, "What about you? Where are you going?"

"Home. Back to Strawberry. I don't know why—I guess because there's no place else to go. Maybe I can get a job in town, waiting tables . . . I don't know."

"Well, we're still travelling the same way then. I reckon we might as well travel together."

Penny got her blankets from the wagon and gave one to Shell. He built a small fire and curled up next to it, wearing his recovered Colt. Penny went a little way up the hill and rolled up.

The night was cold, the stars brilliant, the fire bending in the wind which had risen at dusk. Shell was restless, unable to sleep. After a time he rolled out and boiled some coffee, sipping it as the night drifted past.

"I don't know if I could have turned you in for the reward," Penny said. Shell's eyes lifted to her dark bed. He said nothing. "I don't think Grampa was sure he could do it either. There was that little doubt," she went on.

"You see, Mister Morgan, we had nothing, and it pained Grampa to know he couldn't do for me. I could see it in his eyes as he watched me mending my dress, sometimes while I was scrubbing up the pans in the cabin he would sit there watching, his eyes damp. It didn't matter to me, not really . . . though I would have liked a dress, a chance to go dancing with a man, a bed that didn't poke me when I turned over . . ."

She fell silent. Shell finished his coffee and stretched. Climbing back into his roll he pulled the blanket around his chin.

"Mister Morgan?"

Shell turned his head toward Penny's bed. "What is it?"

"Those women . . . like the one in your hotel room. Is that the kind you favor? The kind you favor most, I mean?"

"Go to sleep," Shell muttered. Then he turned over again and dozed off himself, the fire flickering low.

5.

Viewed from the hills to the south and east, Strawberry wasn't much of a town. A single main street which doglegged in the middle to parallel the railroad track. There were no more than twenty structures lining the street, seven of them of frame construction with false fronts. Four of these, according to Penny, were saloons.

There was a half completed yellow brick building in the center of town, and some civic-minded soul had planted a row of chestnut trees on the south side of the street.

Back a ways from the main street were a handful of shacks. Two or three were adobe, the rest jerry-built from old railroad crates and the like.

"It's not much, is it?" Penny said. "Funny—it always seemed large, exciting, and dangerous somehow when Grampa used to take me down to visit."

"You can bet it's still dangerous," Shell answered.

"Yes." Penny hesitated, not saying something which was on her mind. Perhaps she sensed that she could say nothing which would have an effect on this man. His mind was made up, and that was that. "Luck be with you, then," Penny said. She turned her horse's head and Shell called.

"You're not going into town?"

"Not just yet," she answered. "I've some things at the cabin I must get."

"I'll ride along with you then," Shell said. Surprise registered on Penny's face, but she said nothing.

She led off toward the foothills to the west, Shell following. It was a rugged but beautiful land they crossed. The desert gave way to rocky plateaus which stair-stepped toward the mountains beyond. The earth was iron red, and there was but sparse grass. Here and there Shell saw the tracks of a mule deer or an antelope, so there was game here, probably more in the uplands.

An occasional cedar spread wind flagged limbs toward the east, and in the bottoms there were cottonwoods and sycamores. A few high, fluffy clouds drifted across the azure sky, casting shadows on the warm earth.

They rode up a long, winding gorge, Shell taking in the lay of the land, appreciating the cool breeze which now floated down from the high country.

The rifle shot broke his reverie and he drew his horse up quickly. From a feeder canyon a lone cowboy, tall, needing a shave, rode to meet them. He held a Winchester pointed skyward. Shell's hand rested on the butt of his Colt.

"Miss Dolittle," the cowboy nodded, eyeing Shelter Morgan.

"Sam Yawkey!" Penny was upset. "What in the world are you shooting at? What are you doing away up here anyway."

"A man should stay on his land," Yawkey replied. He smiled crookedly. "I claimed this section here, Miss Dolittle." He pointed with the rifle barrel. "From Big Ford to Tourmaline Peak. The ridgeline to Grizzly Run."

"You filed on this?" Penny asked, looking around. "Why? There's no water, you can't graze cattle?"

"I just sorter took a notion, you might say," Yawkey replied. "You goin' up to your place?"

"Yes. But I won't be staying. Grampa died on the trail. I'm just getting my things. I'll be moving into Strawberry, I guess."

"Your Grampa passed on?" Yawkey took off his battered hat, holding it over his heart. "I'm right sorry, Miss Dolittle. You just go on through this time. The thing is, won't be nobody allowed up this trail from here on out. I can't have folks tramplin' my graze." He shook his head slowly. "I might have to fence it off."

"Well . . ." Penny's nose crinkled up in puzzlement. "Thank you. I'll just be going up this last time."

"And him?" Yawkey nodded at Shelter.

"Just this once," Penny said. "This gentleman escorted me back through the desert."

"I see." Yawkey put his hat back on, rocking it to position. "You got a name, mister?" he asked.

"Sure." Shelter smiled evenly. "Don't everybody?" Then he kneed his horse forward, up the trail, Penny following closely. After they had made the bend, Shell reined up.

"Thanks," he told the girl.

"For what?"

"Well, you sorta covered for me. I escorted you!" Shell laughed. "Only time I was ever trussed to ride escort."

"It's nothing," Penny shrugged. She took off her hat, letting her abundant brown hair fall free. She was thinking of something else and Shell asked her what it was.

"This land." She waved a hand around her. "Who in his right mind would want title to it?"

Shell looked around, appreciating her point of view. Red earth, mostly up and down canyons, with no water at all and nothing but patches of cholla growing anywhere. "There's men that only want to feel they own something," Shell said. "Anything at all. A man will buy a broken gun, a bucket with a hole in it if it's cheap enough. This—he got it for the filing fee, no doubt."

They started on again, at a walk. Penny was not convinced. "Sam Yawkey couldn't work this land if there was anything that could be done with it. He works for Mister Zukor at Slash Z. Besides, you heard him . . . his tongue was so far in his cheek I thought it would poke on through."

"It's a puzzle," Shell shrugged. Yet it did not concern either one of them enough to continue pondering it. Penny only wanted her belongings, to say goodbye to these lonesome hills.

Shell, he only wanted Mister Wes Chambers.

They climbed higher into the red earth canyon, and the wind grew cooler yet. They had nearly reached the grassy, flat uplands when Penny saw something else which was new to her.

A road winding to the high country intersected their own trail. Heavily traveled, by the hoofprints and wagon ruts cut into the trail, it was fenced off with double strands of barbed wire.

"Now that's strange," she told Shell. "That road was never fenced before. And look at the travel."

"Where's it lead?"

"Up to Canyon Rim. That's what my father named it. It's where the old ranch was, our home."

"Before it burned?" Shell asked, recalling that Ben Dolittle had mentioned a ranch fire.

"Yes. My mother and father were killed that night. Grampa saved me."

"Is that still your land?" Shelter wanted to know. Penny smiled ironically.

"No, of course not. Grampa had to sell all of that property. Of course he discussed it with me first. I was only a child, but I knew it had to be done. Slash Z bought it from us, although I've never seen any of their cattle in the highlands. I think Mister

Zukor was doing a favor for us when he purchased it."

"Maybe he's using it now," Shell commented.

"Maybe. It's lovely up there. A view of all the desert, great cedars and rich grass. It could be he's building it up."

The cabin on Grizzly Run was all that Penny had left, and it was little enough. Made of barked logs, chinked with mud, the rear of the house was an old dugout butted against the side of a cliff.

Stepping from the horses Shell said nothing. Penny stood meditatively before the shack, seeing memories, perhaps. Shelter could appreciate it. And he could see how life must have been for a young girl up in these lonely hills, alone with her grandfather, never seeing a neighbor's face, hearing the talk of womenfolks, or catching the eyes of a young buck on her.

"I hate to leave," Penny sighed, "as rough as this place is. Still it was home."

The roof was low, and Shelter ducked going through the doorway. It was as neat as possible under the circumstances, a packed earth floor swept clean, pots hanging neatly from pegs in the wall, the table with a faded blue checked cloth thrown over it.

Penny crossed the room slowly, going to a trunk which she opened. She stood, arms crossed, looking at the contents. "There's really nothing worth taking," she said, and when she turned back to Shell there were tears in her eyes. Angry at herself she turned her back to Shell, wiping her eyes with a knuckle.

Shell rubbed his jaw and shifted uncomfortably. "There a saddle around somewhere? That roan's backbone is rubbing a hole in my britches."

"There are two," Penny sniffed. "In the shed out back."

"I'll saddle them ponies and water 'em. Get what you want," he told her. She only nodded, her back still turned to Shell and he went out, taking a deep breath. He was not good at that sort of situation, and try as he might he had been able to think of nothing comforting to say.

In the shed he found the saddles, worn, patched jobs, and he saddled the horses leading them to the trough where he pumped some water for them. Then he perched on a rail, watching the sky, the mountains, hearing Penny moving around in the cabin, opening and shutting cupboards.

There were a few lazy clouds high in the sky, and now Shell could see a good stand of cedar and pine high on the cliffs where the old ranch house was. A thin tendril of smoke curled into the skies from near there. Perhaps Penny was right about someone moving in again.

"I guess this is it," Penny said.

She had a burlap sack with a few things stuffed in it, a couple of blankets over her arm. She smiled oddly, perhaps ashamed of the poorness of her legacy. Shell took the items and tied them on behind the saddle.

"Ready?" he asked.

"Yes." Penny nodded absently and let her eyes return briefly to the squat, rough cabin, the cliffs rising beyond the house. Then she took the reins

Shell handed her and stepped into the saddle, a small, lonely girl in outsized clothes stepping into a new world.

They rode through the gathering shadows of the deep canyon. The desert was flushed red beyond the gorge. Yawkey was no longer guarding the trail, at least he did not make his presence known.

Strawberry lay spread out before them. A light had already been turned on in one of the buildings. The faint tinkling of a piano drifted through the twilight air to them.

The streets were dark when they hit town. From one of the saloons, the Last Stand, the sound of uproarious laughter flowed forth. "The sheriff's office is at the end of the street," Penny told him in a low voice.

"I'll find it. Do you know where you're going?"

"Mrs. Dawkins runs the restaurant. Her house is behind it. I think she'll give me a job. That's where I'll be if . . ." Penny turned sharply toward him. "You don't have to do this! It's foolhardy, illegal . . ."

"It's all of that," Shell replied calmly. "You take care of yourself."

"Why are you so stubborn!" she demanded in frustration.

"I couldn't say." Shell grinned, "I sure am though, ain't I?"

"Damn!" Penny muttered. She bit at her lower lip and then rode away, toward the Dawkins' house, pausing only to say, "You know where I'll be."

"So long, Penny." Shell walked his horse the

length of the main street, checking the loads in his Colt as he rode. There were few folks out. A cowboy walked a zigzag line down the boardwalk, a stout man in a city suit strode briskly past.

There was a light in the sheriff's office and Shell swung down, leaving his horse untied. He stepped onto the boardwalk and glanced in the window before stepping into the office.

A man with a deputy's badge glanced up from the desk. He had his boots crossed on the desk, a cup of cofee getting cold in his hands. Behind him on the wall was a gunrack and a wanted poster board. Shelter suppressed a smile at seeing his own name in the upper right-hand corner.

"He'p you?" the deputy asked. He was lean and dirty, with lazy, pouched eyes. Shell nodded.

"I'm lookin' for Chambers," Shell replied easily. His eyes shuttled around the bare office, going to the cell where a slack-jawed cowboy was sleeping off a load of booze.

"He ain't here," the deputy said.

"Gone home, has he?"

The deputy eyed Shell dubiously. "You know Wes?"

"I used to run with him," Shelter said.

"He's out of town," the deputy said. "Gone to bring in some prisoners."

"Do you know where?"

"I know." The deputy got to his feet, setting his cup down on the paper-strewn desk. "But that's kinda private information. If you'd just leave me your name, tell me where you'll be stayin'."

"I can't say where I'll be," Shell said evasively,

"I'm just passin' through Strawberry, you might say."

"Do you know your name?" the deputy asked. There was a rough edge to his words now. Something about the tall man struck him wrong.

"Yeah." Shell smiled and turned casually toward the door. Over his shoulder he said, "But you might say that's kinda private information. I'll check back."

Then he nodded and stepped out, closing the door. The deputy's name was Farrell, and he had seen a lot of men. Most were easy to peg. Drifters, cowboys, lawmen—all wore a mark on them, some identifying trait, a cast to the eyes, a way of moving, talking. This man . . . Farrell shook his head, not liking the way he read the blond man.

Farrell walked to the door and opened it, seeing the tall man ride slowly up the street, disappearing gradually into the deep shadows.

He closed the door and went back to his cluttered desk. Once before he had met a man who was cut like this one. He had been a one-armed, cold-eyed man who worked off and on for the army.

A professional scalp hunter.

6.

Shelter put his horse up in the stable, forking some hay himself, adding a dipper of oats. That horse had hauled a wagon halfway from Fort Bowie, and been ridden the rest of the way in. It deserved a breather. There was no one around the stable-just then. Maybe it was supper hour.

By the feeble glare of the lantern light Shelter removed his belt and split the seam with the point of his bowie knife. The gold piece was still there. Twenty bucks he had picked up riding shotgun for

Butterfield. How long it would have to last, there was no telling. But his stomach would not last much longer if he didn't break into it.

He sauntered up the main street of Strawberry, listening to the night sounds. A woman laughed scratchily in a saloon, a glass broke and a muffled curse rolled into the street.

He kept his eye on the shadows, his Colt near to hand. Chambers was supposedly out of town. Maybe not. If he was, there was nothing to do but sit and wait for the man.

Or was there? Turning it over in his mind Shelter considered the possibilities. Here he would be in Chambers' town, surrounded by his people. He would far rather face Chambers on the desert — if he could find out which direction the sheriff was riding.

Shell stepped through the painted door of Mrs. Dawkins' restaurant, finding the room crowded, heavy with the smells of ham frying, fresh coffee and of men. There were two long plank tables and Shell took a seat at the end farthest from the door.

"Help you?" a buxom blond woman of middle years asked. She stood wearily on one foot, pad in hand.

"Whatever's on. Ham and eggs. Coffee."

"We're fresh out of the eggs. Got grits," she suggested.

"That'll be fine," Shell nodded.

The woman walked away, scratching on her pad, and Shell glanced around the room. The men were mostly cowhands, with a teamster here and there, one old man in greasy buckskins and a fellow in a fancy ruffled shirt — a gambler, Shell guessed.

They all had their faces in the trough, and no one as much as glanced back. The waitress brought the ham and grits, returning with a quart pot of coffee minutes later, and Shell dug in.

"Mind if I sit here? It's gettin' a mite crowded." A tall man with worry-drawn lines nodded at the bench and Shelter picked up his hat which rested there, putting it on a knee.

"Come and set," he said amiably.

"Thanks."

He placed his order and sat drumming his fingers on the table. Shelter pushed his plate aside and poured a second cup of coffee.

"Stranger around here?" the man said finally.

"That's right."

"Well, I guess I am rightly. My name's Pilkin." He stuck out a hand which Shell took. The waitress arrived with a steaming plate and Pilkin moved his arms. "I pass through Strawberry," he said around a mouthful of food. "But I'd sure as hell hate livin' here."

"It ain't much," Shell agreed. "You travel, you say?"

"Cattle buyer. Get down once in a while to dicker with Hamilton Zukor — he's Slash Z, over south," Pilkin waved with a fork.

"You know the sheriff here?" Shell asked, stirring his coffee.

"Chambers? Bet your spurs I do. He ain't much either. Suits the town just fine," Pilkin judged. "He's not in town though," he added as an afterthought.

"So I heard."

"You looking for Chambers?" Pilkin asked, lifting an eyebrow.

"Yeah."

"That's kind of like looking for trouble, isn't it?" Pilkin commented. He studied the raw boned, blue eyed man seated next to him carefully and shook his head.

"I suppose it might be," Shell answered. "Depending on who you are."

"He's trouble for anyone," Pilkin said forcefully. "He ain't a friend of yours?" he asked cautiously.

"No. Not exactly."

"I passed him riding down here. He's headin' north again."

"Which trail?" Shell wanted to know.

"Steamboat Wash. But you'll not catch up. He's three days gone."

"But he'll be coming back," Shell said, finishing his coffee. "Mind showin' me where this trail lies?"

"I could . . ." Pilkin again eyed Shelter, trying to make him out. Hesitantly he sketched out the trail on the back of a card.

"I appreciate this," Shelter said.

"It's nothing." Pilkin looked thoughtfully at Shelter, then poked his pencil away in a vest pocket. "Mister," the cattle buyer said when Shell was ready to leave, "I don't know why you want to see Wes Chambers, and I don't want to know. But he's not riding alone. He's got four tough men along. Thought you might want to know."

"Appreciate it," Shell nodded. He walked to the cash register, surprised by a pair of friendly eyes, a familiar smile. Penny Dolittle, her hair pinned up, wearing an apron over a checked gingham dress stood behind the register.

"I wondered . . . I was so worried," she said nervously. She took the gold piece from Shelter, her fingers lingering on his.

"Chambers is out of town," he told her.

"Then we can . . ."

Her face brightened with a smile, but Shelter interrupted her. "I'll be needing to use that roan a while longer, Penny. And I'd appreciate it if you could have a couple of sandwiches made up. Some dried apples and coffee packed for travelling would be fine too."

"You're not leaving! You can't!" Penny objected.

"What is it you want from me, Penny?" Shell asked with a grin. "First you don't want me coming into Strawberry, now you don't want me to leave."

"I don't want you to get hurt!" she said, infuriated by that careless grin of Shelter Morgan's. "I just don't want you hurt."

"Well, we can agree on that," Shell answered. "Will you see to that food?"

Angrily she slapped his change on the counter and spun toward the kitchen, her tiny boots clicking against the floor.

Shell waited for her to return, and when she did she brusquely handed him a large oilcloth wrapped package, turning to the next man in line.

"Penny?"

She counted the other man's change, twice losing count. Her head she kept turned to the counter or to the register. The cowboy beside Shell smiled faintly, looking from Shelter to Penny and back again.

"Guess you're not cuttin' much ice," he cracked.

"No. I guess not." At that Penny's head came up.

"Shell . . ."

"Goodbye, sprout," he said. He put his hand on hers for a moment, winked and walked to the door, her eyes on his broad back.

It was cold outside, the stars bright in a black sky. Two cowboys, fighting for all they were worth, rolled out of the saloon as he passed. Shell side-stepped them and walked to the stable.

The stablehand, a bleary-eyed whip of a man named Jake, let Shell sleep in the hay for two-bits. He had no urge to start up an unknown trail at night, besides he was beat. Plain beat, and it had been a time since he had slept untied. The hay was pungent, prickly, but a damned comfortable bed.

Shelter rolled out with the first light, saddling the roan which seemed to be growing used to the saddle. He took no time for breakfast, but rode northward, the rising sun on his shoulder. As he rode he munched on the sandwich which had been sliced thick, both ham and bread. Only once did he hesitate. On the outskirts of town he thought for just a moment he heard a girl calling his name, and he looked back, but he saw no one, and he heeled the roan forward up the long trail.

The day was dry, clear, the footing sandy beneath the roan's hooves. Shelter let the horse find its own easy pace, and from time to time he even dozed in the saddle, the sun warm on his back.

There was little to worry about. The trail led between surrounding sandy bluffs, willow growing profusely along the bottom. The horse could hardly wander and Chambers was several days away from what Pilkin had said.

He saw no one the day long. Nor much game, but the jackrabbits which were everywhere, pricking their long ears then loping off in a long circle route as Shell approached. A jackrabbit will always run in a circle, trying to get back to home while losing pursuit. A smart pair of dogs have no trouble with a jack, speedy as they are. One will be the runner, the other simply waits, staying at home till jack returns.

Sweat trickled down Shell's throat, the dust filled his nostrils. At midday he found a pond left from winter's rain and he loosened the cinches on the roan's saddle, letting it drink all it wanted as he ate the second sandwich, boiling some coffee to chase it down.

He sat in the meager shade of some willow brush, watching the horse, thinking about Chambers. There had to be a way to cut him loose from his men, take him on alone. If Chambers were flushed would he too run in a circle? A man has to be a fool, Shell thought. Look at him, chasing down this gunman when he knew the odds were as long as Texas.

Yet the memories would not die, memories of friends being gunned down, of Dinkum layin' dead in the Conasauga. Shelter could break off his pursuit at any time. It would be the safe way, maybe the smart way—if there was a way to forget their treachery, their blood letting. But Shelter could not let it die. He was not built that way.

Now they knew he was coming, apparently. Chambers had that wanted poster out. At least the man wasn't sleeping nights.

Shell saddled again and rode, following the wash up past Five Buttes and down onto the flats beyond. The Arizona skies held clear, tinting the sands at dusk with a brief, fiery sunset.

Shell camped a mile above Indian Wells, hunching over a small fire as the night turned cold. Ahead, maybe ten miles off he saw another tiny fire. Chambers? Maybe so.

A nervous excitement ran up Shell's spine, bringing a smile to his lips. He leaned back on one elbow, sipping his coffee, watching that fire for a long while.

Penny came to his thoughts briefly. The baby girl with the hot temper and undergrowed figure. He hoped she was doing well. Maybe she'd find herself a cowboy to take her home.

Dawn came with a rush of color, crimson and flat orange. Shelter was on the trail with first light, his horse sketching a long crooked shadow against the flats.

He rode with more caution now, eyes on the horizon, wanting to spot Chambers before they spotted him. He had been treating the roan carefully, and it seemed to have regained its vigor. Shelter had to hold it back in the cool morning when its native urge to move, to see what lay beyond the next hillrise was strongest.

Midday was sun-bright, a white sun against a

white sky, sapping the strength of man and horse alike.

He saw the clouds of dust long before he could make out the approaching horses and riders. Shelter reined up sharply, eyes squinting against the torrid sun. The cloud was a way off, but growing larger, nearer.

"Whoa there." Shell reined up, patting the roan's neck. "Let's do some climbin'," Shelter said to the horse which pricked its ears with curiosity and blew.

Shell guided the horse up a narrow ravine, climbing to the east. There was a deal of shale on the ravine, and the climbing was rough, yet the roan was game for it.

Cresting out the low hill, Shell halted, studying the flats below. The dust cloud still moved closer. There were plenty of men in that group. Now he could make out three horsemen and nearly a dozen others on foot. Frowning he rode back a way from the rim and ground tethered the pony.

He moved back toward the rim, forcing his way through a tangle of sage and manzanita. Drawing his Colt, Shell scooted on his belly to the very edge of the bluff, watching them as they came.

Chambers . . . he could not make out their faces. Squinting into the fierce sun he tried to penetrate the swirling dust with his vision, yet they were still too far off.

The day was dry, the earth beneath him hot. The dust-screened body of men drew nearer.

Shelter heard the sharp crack of a twig behind him and he spun, but it was too late already. Two men on horseback sat there, each with a rifle levelled at Shelter Morgan.

"Didn't know who that was comin'," Shell bluffed. "Thought I'd better get off the trail."

"Stand up," one of them said.

They wore badges, Shell now saw, and he started to holster his Colt, still running that bluff. "Happy to see you boys. I had some trouble with some men I met on the trail. Rough ones, they were," Shell said, shaking his head. He tried a smile, but that bought nothing from these two.

Hard cases they were, both long-jawed, dark eyed men. They might have been related, though one of them was near bald, the other with a thick stand of crinkly dark hair.

"You want to toss that sidearm away," this one suggested.

"I explained . . ."

"Or do you want to die here?"

"Take it easy," Shell said, holding up a hand. With a sinking feeling in his gut he lifted the Colt gingerly from his holster and tossed it down.

"He's got a knife, Earl," the bald deputy said.

"Ditch that hog-sticker too," the other one told Shell, and he did so.

"Now. Let's get over to your horse and ride on down. We can do it real easy, can't we?" Earl asked, and Shell nodded, reading the warning. Instinct told him these two would have no compunctions about gunning him down.

They waited while he stepped into the roan's saddle, then pointed the trail out to him. Obediently he rode ahead of them, those rifles countering any idea of escape.

"You know," Shell said casually, "there's nothing to this. I told you what happened."

"You'll tell it to the sheriff, friend," Earl said, "if he believes it, you're free to ride off."

"And if he doesn't?"

"If he don't . . . friend, you haven't begun to learn what misery is yet in that case."

7.

He sat there watching as the deputies escorted
Shell toward the halted band of men. For a moment a bitter expression flashed in Wes Chambers'
eyes and curled his thin lips. Shell thought he
might drop a hand to the side gun he wore beneath
the flap of that coat. Instead the mood passed and
Chambers grinned—broadly, and with immense
satisfaction.

"Found him on the rim," Earl said.

"Hello, Captain Morgan," Wes Chambers said,

savoring it. His oily eyes were gleeful as they searched the face of the tall man on the roan.

"Chambers." Shell nodded. "Quite a coincidence, isn't it?"

Chambers burst out laughing. "Oh, yeah. It sure is, Morgan." More soberly he added, "I heard it was a coincidence when you ran into Virg Plum and Twyner down south."

"I've been looking up a few acquaintances from the old days," Shell replied softly. Still he could manage a smile, and that seemed to unnerve Wes Chambers. His eyes flickered to the hills around them.

"Alone are you?"

"I've got about fifty men up there," Shell said, following Chambers' eyes. "Couple of cannon."

"Never lost that wise-ass edge to you, did you?" Chambers spat. "You will, Captain, you will."

Shelter's eyes had gone to the rest of Chambers' band. Six armed men, all mounted, and in front of them a dozen filthy, brutalized prisoners. Three were white, six Indians, the others Mexicans or breeds.

"What do you want to do with him?" Earl asked lazily.

"Get him off that horse," Chambers snapped. "And put these on him." Dipping his hand into his saddlebags he came up with a pair of heavy leg irons. They clanked to the earth at Shell's feet. "I won't have this one running. Not Shelter Morgan."

"Sit down, boy," Earl said roughly, and when it was not quick enough to suit him, he shoved Shell down with the butt of his Winchester.

"Slap them irons on, Luke," Earl said. The second deputy yawned and stepped from his horse as Earl's gun covered Shelter and Wes Chambers' crooked smile widened the more he thought of it.

"What made you think someone was up on that bluff?" Shelter wanted to know. Luke clicked shut an ankle iron painfully and Shell winced. "You got no touch, Luke."

"Shut up," the deputy growled.

Chambers was silent until Shell was securely chained, then he answered the question Shell had put to him. "I didn't know nobody was up there. I always use outriders. A lot of times a prisoner'll have friends, family that wants to break him loose. The Injuns especially," Chambers tugged his hat lower. "This time, I just happened to be real lucky."

"Now?" Luke asked, straightening up slowly.

"Now?" Wes smiled, and it was an ugly smile, "Get him in line with the rest of these convicts."

Shell stood with difficulty and Luke put a rifle muzzle in his back. "Move," he said and Shell took a step. But Earl had been standing on the leg irons and they came up short, Shell slamming to the hot earth, his face thudding against a palm sized rock.

Slowly he got to his feet, blood streaming from his nose. He started to pick up his hat, but Earl placed a foot on it.

"Now, Captain," Wes Chambers said savagely. "we begin playing by the rules. Or we don't play anymore. You move when I say move, and if you can't move fast enough I'll have a man behind you kicking at your ankles. If you fall we'll ride over you; fight and you're dead!" He levelled a finger at Shell. "You hear me, because that's the way it's going to be."

Wes Chambers' chest was rising and falling with excitement. Now he slowly lowered that finger and turned to Earl who was beside him, in the saddle again.

"Let's move 'em, Earl."

They trudged southward, the sun searing Shell's hatless head, the dust stirred up by the horses choking him. Twice he fell before learning a waddle gait which allowed him to keep up in those irons.

Silently they walked, and their faces were hardly human. Washed out by the clinging dust, hopeless faces which stared vacantly across the desert flats. They were indeed heading back toward Strawberry, or so it appeared. But why all of these men? Shell asked the Mexican next to him in a low voice.

"*Quien sabe?*" he shrugged, his black eyes flickering to the nearest guard, Luke.

"I've seen that jail in Strawberry," Shell muttered. "It wouldn't hold half of us."

"At least you've seen Strawberry," a white haired man on the other side said. "I've never even been through the place. What the hell are they taking me there for!"

"Shut up, Swede!" Luke said.

Still they moved forward, their tongues wooden, legs like lead. No one offered them water and none of the prisoners dared to ask.

Finally they rested. Chambers and his deputies boiled coffee and broke out some beef which they fried in bacon grease. The prisoners passed a cup of water around. Swede took it greedily, gulping the saving water.

A hand reached out and jerked the cup away, tearing it from Swede's fingers. A heavy man with a black beard raised a fist to Swede's face.

"Damn you! It's all we're likely to get," the big man said savagely. "Pass it on."

"I'm sorry . . . I didn't."

"Shut up." The big man took a sip, passing it to the Mexican next to him.

"That's Jack Riley," Swede whispered to Shell. "He's poison."

Shell casually glanced at Riley. Shell had heard the name mentioned before. Jack Riley had killed four men that they knew of, all brutally, without the slightest trace of emotion. He had huge, gnarled hands, and massive shoulders. It was said he favored twisting a man's neck until it snapped.

The Indians sat to one side, accepting no water. Five of them, together with one of the half-breeds sat in a group, arms around their knees.

One sat alone, eyes flinty, mouth set. He held his head proudly. "Him too," Swede said nudging Shell, "stay away from him. His name's Banquero. Cousin to that renegade Chiricahua, Thumb."

"Heard of him," Shell replied softly. When he glanced again at Banquero, he found the Apache's eyes staring back hard.

Of the other Indians Shell believed one to be a Ute, one a Navajo, the others Arapaho. The other white man was little more than a kid. A dark haired, sober looking man with only patches of dark whisker on his sunburned face.

"Who's that?" Shell wanted to know.

"Don't know much about him," Swede shrugged. "He was in the lock-up when I got to Steamboat. Calls himself Frank Tyler, but I think it's a phony."

"On your feet!" Luke strolled among the prisoners, chewing a piece of beef slowly, with taunting relish. "On your feet and shut your mouths."

He paused in front of Shelter, casting a shadow. He smiled briefly and then his boot shot out with all of the deputy's force behind it. It caught Shell on the point of the chin and he slammed backward, his mouth filling instantly with hot, salty blood.

"I mean on your feet *now*!" Luke said, chuckling. Shell got to hands and knees and then stood, his fists clenched. "Go ahead," Luke said. "Take a poke at me, Morgan."

Slowly Shell's fists unclenched and Luke turned away laughing. From there Shelter could see Wes Chambers grinning as Luke strode back toward him.

"Take it easy," Swede said, "or you'll never live to see a cell."

Shell wiggled a loose tooth and spat out a mouthful of blood. Jack Riley was watching silently. "I don't figure I'll ever see a cell anyway," Shelter told them. "The sheriff's got a big grudge against me, and an itch to blow my brains out."

Slowly they clambered to their feet and formed again into ragged ranks, marching southward. The shadows grew long, Shell's feet were on fire, his ankles chafed raw, his thighs cramped, yet they did not stop.

79

Swede looked helplessly at Shell, opened his cracked, blistered lips to say something which never came out. Then he toppled forward, falling in the dust among the tramping feet.

The prisoners marched around him, over him. Shell had halted, kneeling beside Swede who was ashen, his pulse shallow.

"Leave him!" Earl shouted, circling back on his horse. He had a rifle in his hand, and he repeated his command.

"He'll die," Shell said in exasperation. "If we could stop for a while . . . it's near dark anyway."

"Damn you Morgan!" Earl yelled. He rode near to Shell, his horse's hooves cutting the sand around Swede. "Get up and get moving!"

"Go to hell!"

Earl spun his horse, the rifle coming down, but Shelter was first. He got his hands under Earl's right stirrup and with all of his strength he shoved up, unseating the deputy.

Earl slammed to the ground and got up livid with rage, levering a cartridge into the chamber. Shell stood watching him, unable to move. Earl raised the rifle to his shoulder, but at that moment another horse was bearing down on them and Shell felt the violent impact of the horse's shoulder against his body.

He was bowled over, landing sharply on a shoulder which filled with fiery pain. Wes Chambers sat his horse between Shelter Morgan and his furious deputy.

"Put it down, Earl."

"He back-talked me. Came after me. You made

the rules! A man does that, he dies."

"I don't want Morgan going out so easy," Chambers said. There was more savagery in his words than in those of Earl. An animal longing to see Shelter suffer, a need to watch him writhe, dying a bit at a time, had bored itself into Wes Chambers' ugly mind.

Slowly Shell came to his feet, holding his battered shoulder. Earl turned his horse angrily, riding to the point.

Swede was on his knees, gasping for breath, the evening shadows blurring his pain-wracked face. Wes let his horse take another step forward, then he said to Shell—"You want to save this man, you carry him."

Swede shook his head miserably. "It's all right, he can't . . ."

"I said carry him! If you want him to live. Otherwise I'm going to put a bullet in his head and leave him here."

"I'll carry him," Shell panted. "Swede?"

"You can't."

"I'll let you know when I can't," Shell said mildly. He gave the man a hand up and then took him piggy-back, his shoulder burning with the pain.

"Now . . . get moving, Morgan. Don't stop again, I'm warning you. It'll be the last stop if you do."

Shelter nodded, and he stepped off, slogging behind the other prisoners, Luke's rifle on them. "I'm sorry," Swede puffed.

"It's all right. It'll be dark soon," Swede answered. "They'll have to let us stop. By morning you'll be good as new."

"I'll never be good as new," Swede said. "Not if this keeps up much longer. Damn the cards," he muttered. "Damn the whiskey and the cards!"

They made camp that night in the sandy hills north of Strawberry. From there they could see the twinkling lights in the town, imagine the drinking, the women.

Earl and Luke had broken out a spider-like arrangement of chain, and with the prisoners sitting in a close circle, each man's leg irons had been attached to it, binding them all together.

Still there was no food—obviously Chambers did not even carry supplies for the prisoners. Swede was recovering some in the coolness of evening. He lay flat on his back, watching the stars, grateful that he had lived to see the sun go down.

A large part of this still puzzled Shelter. Swede, for instance, had never been in Strawberry—or so he said. How was it that he came under Chambers' jurisdiction? There were no facilities for this number of prisoners in the town. Why such a large number of men together?

"Tomorrow we'll be in Strawberry," Swede muttered. "In jail. I never thought a cell would look so good. I'm not strong, Morgan. This sun will kill me."

"They'll not keep me in that jail long," Jack Riley growled. The big man was scowling toward the deputies, clustered around their campfire. "And when I get out, I'll kill every man-jack of them. I swear it."

"They never tried me," Swede objected. "Never

tried me. I swear I didn't bottom deal that man. He was just running bad luck." He looked to Shell, eyes pleading for belief.

"I guess I was tried a long ways back," Shell commented to himself. "By a jury of my peers."

"They goin' to hang you?" Jack Riley asked.

Shelter shrugged. "I expect so, unless Chambers can think of a slower way."

"They were goin' to hang me," Riley said, "in Steamboat. But they put it off the morning they was to do it. Then Chambers picked me up. I never seen Strawberry in my life," the big man said strongly. "But it's got to look better than a gallows."

Frank Tyler sat silently listening. The kid hadn't said two words all day. Maybe he was just trying to stay out of trouble. Now he did speak.

"What about the Indians?" he asked. "What right does Chambers have to lock up Indians?"

"And the Mexican—that's Federal jurisdiction," Riley said with the knowledge of one who was intimate with the law and its workings.

"We'll find out soon enough, I guess," Swede said wearily. He lay back, shutting his eyes.

"We'll find out," Shelter agreed. "I'm not so sure we'll like the answer though."

They were up and moving before dawn, marching on blistered, swollen feet, their vision blurry from lack of food, from the dust and sun. Swede could manage on his own now, though his gait was unsteady, and another full day in the sun might be fatal to the gambler.

The sun, glaring, rose red dawned within the

83

hour, bringing an already intense heat. They walked the sandy, airless washes between surrounding hills, struggling for breath.

There was no stopping, nor slowing.

"How far?" Swede panted, clutching Shelter's arm desperately. "How much longer?"

"I don't know," Shell muttered back.

Jack Riley was near enough to hear and the killer put in hotly, "Why the hell don't you know? You said you just rode out of Strawberry?"

"I did," Shelter shrugged, looking around at the unfamiliar hills, the high mesa in the distance. "Thing is, Riley, we aren't heading for Strawberry. Not now."

Riley's jaw twitched angrily. Swede's face fell to disconsolate frustration. Frank Tyler moved nearer to Shelter as they trudged up a long, rocky ravine.

"What you said back there," the kid puffed, "about not going to Strawberry. Was it true?"

"It's true. We swung right past the town," Shell replied.

"Damn," the kid breathed. "That sinks it."

Shell glanced at the kid. "You had folks that were going to bust you out of this?"

"Sort of . . . I had every reason to expect it . . . in Strawberry. Now . . ." the kid shrugged and kept on moving, his face set, eyes discouraged.

They were in the long gorge an hour, sliding back, scrambling upward on a trail never meant for a man, but when they topped out, high in a sawtoothed collection of hills, Shell was able to see exactly where they were and he muffled a slow, curious oath.

"What's up?" Jack Riley sagged beside Shell, panting from the climb. "Know where we are now?"

"I know, but I don't understand it," Shell told the black bearded murderer. They sat in the iron red hills to the west of Grizzly Run, not far from where Penny Dolittle's cabin sat, near where the cowboy had shaken them down.

"I don't see a damned thing," Riley snapped.

"There's nothin' to see," Shelter told him. "These hills are empty. But there's men watching the trails in."

From the corner of his eye Shelter saw some movement. Slow, measured movement. It was the Navajo. Chambers was standing on the other side of the clearing with his deputies, talking in a low voice, and the Navajo was going to make his try, irons or not.

Shelter tried not to look directly at the Indian, not wanting to tip the guards. All of them turned their heads away, but every eye watched secretly as the Navajo, creeping crablike, the irons gathered up in one hand, eased toward the rim of the gorge.

If he could make it over the lip, he had a chance. Maybe the deputies would not even notice his absence, or the Navajo had the second chance of getting a head start down that rock strewn canyon where a horse was little advantage.

Ever so quietly the Navajo moved away, his obsidian eyes alert as an animal's. No one else as much as breathed when Earl's head came suddenly around and he looked directly at Shelter Morgan, not seeing the Navajo who was some fifty feet off now, flat against a slight depression.

Earl's head turned back toward Chambers and the Indian got stealthily to his feet. He took three quick steps.

It was a slight sound, but a distinctive one. The iron chain rang against a rock on the ground and Earl's head came around again, sharply just as the Navajo slipped over the rim.

With a shout Earl charged for the rim, Luke and Chambers following. Shell got to his feet, watching as the Navajo scuttled down the chute, madly climbing over boulders, trying for freedom.

Earl's rifle went to his shoulder and he snapped off a shot. It missed. The Navajo ran on, tumbling down the ravine, clawing to his feet, running again. Another hundred yards . . . he might make it if he could get out of range.

Shell held his breath. Earl sat on the ground, taking a cross-legged position, the sling of his rifle around his arm. Slowly he took his bead and squeezed off.

The shot racketed down the long canyon, and a second later they saw the Navajo jerk upright, slap at his back, half turn and fall. They could see him twitching, hear Earl jack another cartridge into the Winchester, and then he fired again and the Navajo lay still against the hot red earth.

Earl turned, a smug expression on his lips. He let his eyes fall on Banquero who stood glaring savagely at him, then on Shelter Morgan whose blue-gray eyes were unreadable.

"You go ahead, Morgan. You make your run too, if you like. *That* would give me pleasure—putting one in your back."

"Get 'em up," Chambers said angrily. "Get 'em up and get 'em moving. They don't need to rest if they've still got the energy to run!"

"I can't . . ." it was Swede who panted an objection. The gambler was waxen, unsteady on his feet.

"You can," Chambers snapped. "Move it now, old man, or you can join the Indian in the canyon."

Chambers spun his chestnut horse around and led off down the hill. Swede looked helplessly at the others and then staggered forward. Shelter stood a moment longer on the rim, studying the dead Navajo below.

"You want to go down there, Morgan?" Earl asked acidly.

"No." Shelter shook his head and began moving. "It's just a matter of time, Earl," he muttered. "A matter of time before *you* end up layin' dead in some empty canyon."

They moved deeper into the iron red hills, seeing nothing but the earth beneath their feet, the sweating back of the man in front of them.

Finally Shelter found himself on a familiar trail—the one he had ridden the day before with Penny Dolittle. Only now there was a wooden fence across the road. Chambers halted his weary band.

Down from the canyon rode Sam Yawkey and another man who also rode a Slash Z pony. Both men carried Winchester repeaters.

"Howdy, Sheriff!" Yawkey called from across the gate. "On schedule. Got a new batch for us, have you?"

"That's right," Chambers nodded.

"An even dozen—didn't lose none this trip, huh?"

"Lost one, gained one," Chambers said, nodding at Morgan.

"The man with no name," Yawkey said. "He was poking around up here yesterday. With that Dolittle brat."

"You aren't serious?" Wes Chambers said, staring worriedly at Shelter Morgan. "He can't know anything."

"I don't know about that, Wes. All I know is he was damn sure here."

That really bothered Chambers; Shell could read that in the sheriff's oily eyes. Shelter knew nothing besides what he was learning just now, but Chambers couldn't know that.

The thing that bothered Shell was that Penny would also be involved in this, probably. If Chambers thought Shell was snooping around, he might believe Penny Dolittle was his accomplice.

Shell said nothing, looking back flatly at Chambers whose eyes were still curious. "I'll have to look into that," Chambers said. "It could be somebody's wise."

Sam Yawkey had unlocked the gate without stepping from the saddle. Now he backed his horse away, swinging it wide.

"Get moving," Earl grunted. To Luke he said from the side of his mouth. "I've had enough of this bunch. I need me a whisky and a woman."

Ahead they moved, walking the long canyon until they came to the second gate, at the feeder canyon. Luke unhooked the barbed wire strands from the post and threw the gate aside.

They plodded on, moving toward Canyon Rim where the old Dolittle ranch house had been, where Shelter had seen smoke on the day before. The trail curled around the outer face of the mountain, and looking out across the desert Shell could admire the awesome panorama of the raw land. Red earth and yellow sand spread beneath a flawless blue crystal sky. Climbing higher they could make out the stands of cedar and pine high on the mountain slopes, a green velvet grassland spacing two up-thrust peaks. And a gaping black hole carved into the side of the mountain.

8.

Laboring heavily the chain gang was herded together on a nearly circular, grassless section of the valley floor. There was a large, nearly completed frame house in the shadows of the north peak, but they were kept well away from it.

Shell sat wearily on the earth, Swede dropped beside him, going flat on his back to gasp for breath. Luke and Earl stood guard over them while Wes Chambers rode to the house which was fenced, guarded.

"That's it," Frank Tyler said bitterly.

"What?" Jack Riley was dripping sweat, his beard was matted with perspiration and dirt. The big man was mad, and young Frank Tyler flinched under the badman's searing gaze.

"It's a mine," Tyler said, lifting his chin toward the gaping hole carved into the side of the south peak, "and we're the miners."

"Be damned!" Riley muttered.

Looking closely at the cavern above them Shell could now see signs of activity. A mule drawn cart stood before the mine entrance. A man moved methodically doing something Shell could not make out at that distance.

"Slave labor," Shell said slowly and Tyler nodded.

"The bastards," Riley spat.

"Damned smart," Swede said sitting slowly up. "Who the hell would ever report this to the law? Saying a man could escape—could you see Jack Riley walking into the marshal's office to complain?"

"They'd have a loop around my neck by morning," Riley agreed ruefully. "I'd keep running . . ."

Wes Chambers was returning on foot. With him were three other men. Two were obviously guards, fighting men. The third man wore a pearl-gray suit and white shirt.

They walked slowly around the prisoners like buyers at a cattle auction, their conversation detached, cold.

"A decent batch, Chambers."

"Nothing but healthy ones this trip, Mister

Zukor," Chambers said. "Look 'em over."

"I can see, I can see," the fat man said impatiently. "What about him?" his finger jabbed at Swede who cringed from it as if it could kill.

"He's a throw-in. He cheated the wrong man at cards. Fainer wanted to teach him a lesson."

"I see." Zukor shrugged and said something else which Shell was not listening to. *Fainer!* Wes Chambers had said Fainer wanted to teach Swede a lesson. *Colonel* Fainer?

"Who got you into this, Swede?" Shelter said, grabbing the man's arms so hard that it hurt him. "Chambers said a man named Fainer was behind this. Charles Fainer?"

"I don't know his first name," Swede said. "A tall man, brown eyes and a scar on his cheek. Kind of a hawk nose, I guess you'd say. Wears a narrow mustache." Swede looked at Shell whose eyes were distant, thoughtful. "Why, you know him?"

"I know him. A man I trusted once. I looked up to him, Swede, but he was low born, a back stabber. A real first-class back stabber."

"He ain't changed," Swede said, shaking his head dismally. "Hell, he threw down a hundred bucks and I covered it. A man can't help dealing himself a better hand time to time."

"Fainer's a gambler?" Shell asked, puzzled.

"Not so's you'd notice. Hell, man, he's a territorial judge!"

A judge—Shell smiled despite himself. So that was the deal. Fainer remanding prisoners to Wes Chambers whether or not their crimes—real or pretended—had been committed in Chambers' jurisdiction. The prisoners were then transported to Zukor's mine, all at a tidy profit for everyone involved.

And Zukor—how clean could he be anyway? It made Shell wonder about the fire which had burned out the Dolittles, leaving Penny an orphan. Zukor would have waited a time before moving onto the property, enough time to make it seem that his offer had been made only out of compassion for Penny.

It stunk—through and through. The longer Shell thought about it, the madder he got. What really tore at his guts was knowing that he would never be able to do a thing about it. Fainer, Chambers and Zukor would go on living as respectable men, raking in the illegal profits, caring little who else suffered, died.

"You men get to your feet," Zukor said loudly. "Your quarters are over there. As you can see the barracks has not yet been constructed, and it can get very cold up here. *You* will build your own barracks, and if you have any sense you will build quickly and well before winter sets in."

That night they were chained to a thick oak tree stump, the spider chain again being used. They were not alone on the mountain. At sundown a wagon rolled down from the mine and a dozen men fell from it in exhaustion.

Caricatures of men, they were. Scarecrows somehow taken motion. Vacant eyes swept over Shell and the others. Haggard faces, broken hands. Dressed in rags, they were marked with burns and bruises.

One man alone had retained his vitality. A mammoth of a man, long gray hair to his shoulders, a square chin and barrel chest, he surveyed the newcomers silently. At last they heard him say to another miner, "Look at 'em—think they've been through hell and they're still in heaven."

The evening meal was served fifteen minutes later. Scraps of salt pork and a handful of beans floating in some murky, tasteless broth.

Tyler took his ladleful from the guard, tasted it and felt his stomach turn over. He put it aside rather than eat it. A big hand shot out and they turned their heads to see the gray haired giant pour the slop into his own bowl.

"Don't be queasy about it, lads," he said, slurping it down. "Don't eat this, you don't eat nothin'. Eat nothin'," he winked, "you die."

Shelter tasted his, felt a revulsion raise the bile in his gut, held his breath and drank it to the dregs, recognizing that what the big man had said was true. There might be little enough nutrition in the gruel, but at least there was moisture to replace that lost on the desert. Shell had seen men die—slowly, miserably, through dehydration, and he had no intention of going out that way.

Swede gagged his down then lay back, choking on the foul stew.

"They may as well shoot me now if this is their food," Jack Riley muttered.

"You're lucky," the giant said ironically. Riley's black eyes flashed and the big man explained, "it's Sunday."

The night was cool and they slept uneasily, uncomfortably. At first light they were rousted out roughly by three guards. Sour looking men with hard features, their leader wore a black handlebar mustache. His name was Dent, and the older prisoners told Shell that he was named right—he would as soon dent your skull as smile, and he carried a hickory club for that purpose.

They were stacked into the wagon and driven to the mine where they got their first look at the operation. Zukor was tapping an irregular vein of gold, stripping it free of the quartz in a huge ore crusher. How he was refining it, or where it was shipped, they had no idea.

Dent stood before them, his hickory club in his hands, two armed men at his side.

"You boys think you've had it rough up till now. Maybe you have, but it'll be rougher if you don't learn to live with the rules. Make a break, you die. Talk back, you taste the club. Step out of line and you're begging for worse than you've dreamed possible."

Briefly then they were given their assignments. Swede and Torres, the Mexican, were to return to work on the bunkhouse along with one of the old-timers. Jack Riley and Duncan, the gray haired giant, would work the ore-crusher. They had the bulk for it. Frank Tyler would load them.

The Indians, Shell and the rest of the old hands would be in the shafts themselves.

"That all right with you, Mister Morgan?" Dent asked sharply.

"Yes," Shell answered with surprise.

"Good. Because I've been told you like to make

trouble. I have one word for you . . . don't!"

"Don't even look cross-eyed at him," Shell was told later. "He kills and likes it."

Corson was this man's name, one of the old hands, assigned to show Shell and the others the ropes. He was a man of middle years, wiry, with a trace of Texas accent.

Scaling a jerry-built wooden ladder Shelter followed Corson to a ledge which protruded some thirty feet above the ground.

"Winds down and around to the right," Corson pointed, crouching before the cavern entrance. "There's a fork to the left, but it's a dead end. Vein fizzled on us. Watch your head, it's all low. Most of the day you'll be crawlin'. Best to tear up your shirt, anything to pad your knees with."

Shell took his advice and took his shirt off then and there. The one breed who spoke English, a squat man called Jim Fox, translated for the others. Banquero alone refused to follow suit.

He stood on the edge of the ledge, arms crossed, haughtily staring at the guards below. The Chiricahua liked none of this and his hard-lined face showed it.

"Fox?" Shell nodded. "Best tell the man if he don't work he'll die."

Jim Fox shook his head slightly. "He knows this. "He will not be a slave for any man. The Chiricahua must be free."

"Tell him he'll live to see freedom. Tell him he's going about this wrong."

Hesitantly Fox spoke to the Apache. Banquero's eyes went to Shell's and locked there. A rapid spate

96

of Apache followed. Fox turned back to Shelter and shrugged.

"He says, 'Will Blue Eyes take these chains from me? Will Blue Eyes set Banquero free?' " Fox translated. The mockery in Banquero's words was obvious.

"Leave the savage," Corson said. "If we don't get our butts into the hole, we'll all be in for it."

Corson was right, yet Shelter saw something below which made up his mind. One of the guards, the one called Depew, was lifting his rifle under Dent's directions, and he was drawing a bead on Banquero.

The Apache knew what was happening, but he had made his decision—death rather than slavery. Dent would not hesitate to shoot to kill. A slave who will not work is a debit, a worthless hunk of live meat.

"Banquero!"

"Leave him, Morgan!" Corson pled.

Depew's rifle was at his shoulder. Banquero, arms crossed stared defiantly down. Depew fired and Shelter, who had moved a split-second earlier, slammed into Banquero, knocking him aside as a bullet whined off the face of the mountain.

Together they tumbled to the ground and Banquero struck out furiously, his knee driving against Shell's groin. Shell had known it was coming, however, and he rolled just slightly, Banquero's knee glancing painfully off Shelter's thigh. The Apache angrily drove the heel of his hand against Shell's chin, forcing Shell's head back.

Shell slapped out with his hand, breaking the

lock of Banquero's arm at the elbow, and his head came free. Lifting a fist Shell landed a hammering blow on Banquero's jaw and the Indian sagged limply, out cold.

Corson looked frantically from the scuffle to the guards below.

"What's going on, Corson!" Dent's voice called.

"Nothing . . ." he looked at the unconscious Apache, and at Shell who was struggling to his feet. "Nothing at all! He decided to work."

Jim Fox gave Shell a hand at drawing Banquero inside the mine shaft. They dragged him some fifty feet inside the low chamber, Fox nervously watching Morgan's eyes by the dim candlelight.

"You should not have done this," Fox panted. "You have made an enemy of Banquero."

"They were going to shoot him down," Shelter objected.

"Yes. He knew that. He accepted it." Fox shook his head unhappily. "Now, Morgan, you may have to kill the Apache—or be killed yourself."

The day was endless misery. Scuttling through the narrow shafts like rats they picked the gold laden quartz from the stone, loading it onto primitive drays which were dragged back to the mine entrance and emptied into the baskets of men who carried the heavy loads down the ladders to the ore crusher where Duncan and a bare-chested Jack Riley labored.

By midday the heat in the shafts was unbearable. Shell was working as a hauler, drawing the sledge which weighed all of two hundred pounds behind him as he crawled on bloody hands and knees through the low, torchlit shaft.

Perspiration rolled down his face and chest, soaked through his pants. It had to be a hundred and thirty degrees, and the air so stale and dust clotted that he could hardly catch a breath.

Only the anticipation of the clear air at the end of the shaft kept him going. For a brief minute while the ore was unloaded, he was able to drink in the fresh, clean air, the sunlight so bright it burned his eyes after the darkness within.

Shell stood while the Indians loaded their baskets with the white quartz, stretching his back, looking into the far, unfettered distances. If he took too long Depew or one of the others would take a step or two forward, unlimbering their rifles; then he would turn rapidly and crawl back into the black bowels of the mine.

He passed Fox going in. The breed was having a time of it. His face was black with soot and dust and weirdly lighted by the flickering torchlight, he looked only half-human. *Do I look like that?* he wondered.

It was only the first day. How long would it be before they were buried in this shaft, replaced by fresh slaves?

Shell waited at a wide spot in the tunnel, letting Fox come past. The breed whispered as he drew abreast: "Banquero. He waits for you."

Shell nodded, his eyes going to the shaft beyond. The Apache had been working with a short handled pick beside Corson, deliberately, bitterly, working his frustration out. Now perhaps his frustration had found a new target.

Shelter moved ahead, crouched low, his empty sledge behind him. Now he could see the flickering glare of torchlight from the end of the shaft. He had first to make the elbow bend then move another hundred feet to the tail end of the shaft where Corson and the Apache had been working.

Yet if Banquero was waiting . . . the bend was the obvious place. Cautiously Shelter moved ahead, eyes alert. His hands were slick with perspiration, his heart hammered heavily.

He was at the bend now and Shelter stopped. Picking up the dray, he carried it in front of him like a shield.

The torch went out. A shadow lunged toward Shell and he saw the flash of steel. With all of his strength Shelter thrust out with the heavy oaken dray and he felt a vicious blow, that of iron meeting wood as the Indian's pick shivered the sledge in his hands.

Someone had relighted the torch and as the light flared up Shelter saw Banquero's face. The Apache was trying to free the pick. Failing that, he lunged at Shelter barehanded, his dark, lean face a mask of fury.

Shell lifted a knee and half turned away as Banquero flew into him. The knee caught Banquero low in the abdomen, driving the breath out of him, but as Shelter turned to rise, the Apache's iron grip locked on Shell's collar bone, dragging him back, the Indian's fist falling hard against Shell's jaw.

Shelter, flat on his back, stabbed out with a stiff left hand which grazed Banquero's temple. The Apache ducked and his hands, vise-like and incredibly strong, went to Shelter's throat.

Gasping for wind, fighting the lock the Apache had on him, Shelter hooked a right twice to Banquero's ribs. The second blow cracked a rib and Banquero's head went back in anguished pain. But his hands did not release the deadly grip on Shelter's throat.

Desperately Shell winged the right again, catching the Apache low, near the kidney and again he banged out with the left. This time it landed flush and the Indian's head snapped back, the grip momentarily slackening.

Shell lifted a knee hard, then managed to get both his arms beneath Banquero, shoving hard. The Apache was tossed over Shell's head, landing with a grunt. Shelter scrambled to his feet but Banquero was already up.

The man was cat-quick, skilled. Banquero lashed out with a kick, but slowed by the irons it passed harmlessly as Shell crouched and jabbed twice at Banquero's bobbing head.

Banquero pulled away from a thundering right from Shelter Morgan, then dove. He locked his forearm under Shell's chin, his right arm behind his back. He pushed back and up, trying to break Shelter's neck.

They were locked together now, their perspiration-slick bodies glistening in the torchlight. Banquero's face was only inches from Shelter's face and Morgan could read the scorn, the deadly intent in the Apache's black eyes.

Desperately Shell drove a knee at the Chiricahua's groin, but Banquero blocked it with his own knee. Shell slammed his right again and again against Banquero's ribs, but the man seemed made of stone, his relentless pressure against Shell's throat strangling.

Shell relaxed completely, briefly, then slammed an overhand right against Banquero's face. The Indian reeled slightly and Shell again exploded with a right. Banquero stumbled, swayed, and they slammed to the earth, falling across the dray.

When they came to their feet again, Banquero had the handle of the broken pick in his hand. Slowly they circled, crouched low, eyes animal, every nerve set, every muscle tensed.

Banquero lunged, tried to strike the telling blow with that pick handle, but the roof of the cavern was too low, and the handle thudded off the rock over head.

Morgan had been coming in with the motion by Banquero, and the Apache was wide open to a devastating hook which snapped his head to one side. Morgan stepped in, seeing Banquero falter, and he banged away with chopping rights and lefts, working him up and down.

Banquero had done a deal of fighting, but always with axes or knives. He was no boxer. Shell hooked twice to Banquero's painful ribs then went upstairs to the jaw again and the Chiricahua staggered back, hands covering his face.

Shelter moved relentlessly forward, uppercutting the Indian with his right then chopping again to the kidneys. Frustrated, bloodied, Banquero dropped his hands and with a scream of rage lunged at Shell.

That was exactly what Shelter had been waiting for. The Indian's jaw was wide open and he caught him coming in. He caught him flush and Shell could feel the force of the blow, thrown with not only his arms, but with chest, hips, thighs, shiver his own body.

Banquero toppled to the earth, face first, tried to rise on twitching, rubbery muscles and gave up, falling back, bloodied, beaten.

Shelter turned away, gasping for breath in the furnace-like heat of the mine shaft. He was dripping wet, and each breath was like filling the lungs with jagged glass.

He sagged against the wall of the tunnel, hands limp at his sides. Corson was there, watching worriedly, and Jim Fox.

Banquero slowly rolled over and got to a sitting position. He tried to rise, but he didn't have it in him, he sat there, face puffed and bloody, glowering at Morgan.

Shell took a step forward, blinked the perspiration from his eyes and said to Fox, "Tell Banquero this: I will take him out of this place. Blue-Eyes will lead Banquero to freedom. I swear it!"

9.

The days passed in endless progression. There was no reality but the mine shafts, the darkness and heat. Winter was approaching, but they scarcely noticed the change.

Their day began before daybreak with a hurried meal of thin gruel, beans or sourdough with an occasional chunk of fatty beef. The bunkhouse was nearly complete. Of rough timber, Swede and Torres vowed it was air tight and would prove warm when the snows came.

They worked until their muscles ached and then they worked again, growing hard, dirty, savage. They thought only of escape, yet escape never offered itself. The leg irons seldom were off, and then they were under guard. Late in September the padlocks, some of which were rusting, were removed from the chains and iron pins were driven in to secure the irons still better.

They rubbed grease on their ankles, when it could be found, but the relief was minimal. Not a man among them did not dream of the day those chains would be removed. For some, that day came when they were buried. Two of the Indians had died—Fox said of broken hearts, though to Shelter it looked mighty like scurvy.

Banquero worked silently, sullenly, in the ever deepening shafts, his eyes lifting tauntingly to Shelter when they met. Shell was coming to regret the passionate vow he had made the Apache warrior. Perhaps Banquero never had believed it. He believed it less, certainly, as the months slipped away.

It was raining a heavy drizzle the first evening the wagons brought the prisoners home to their completed bunkhouse. Torres seemed proud, Swede only concerned.

"Now there's only the hard labor, isn't there?" he asked Shell. "The mine." He lifted his eyes to the red mountain which was obscured by the shifting veil of rain. "It'll kill me, Morgan. You—you look strong, leather tough from it. Me . . ." he shrugged sadly.

Shell slapped Swede's back and smiled with an

encouragement he did not feel. "You'll make it, Swede. Talk to Dent—them shafts need shoring up awful bad. Maybe he'll let you put some timbers in there now that you're a carpenter."

"They don't care if that tunnel collapses on the lot of us," Corson said, drinking from the dipper.

"No. But they care that it will take time to dig us back out," Shell reminded him. "It can't hurt to have a word with Dent."

"No?" Jack Riley boomed a sarcastic laugh. He parted his matted black hair to show them a lump and a jagged split in his scalp. "*I* had a word with Dent. He answered with the hickory. If I ever get loose . . ."

They stood in the rain waiting for Dent to arrive and unlock the door which was iron-strapped, double bolted on the outside.

"It'll be a dream getting out of the cold," Frank Tyler said softly. "Look what we've sunk to . . . thinking they've done us a favor when all they want is to keep us alive through the winter."

"I was never thinkin' they did me a favor," Shell said. His head lifted slowly and he blinked in astonishment. "Look." He pointed toward an arriving buckboard. "You talk about your dreamin'!"

"No!" Jack Riley leaned on Shell's back, those massive hands on Morgan's shoulders as he gaped.

"Damn me for a Yankee," Corson breathed slowly.

The buckboard was being driven slowly toward the house where a column of smoke lifted to the gray skies. Two strapping bay geldings trotted easily before it and on the seat, holding a black umbrella, was a woman.

"Is it?" Duncan said.

"I've heard of 'em," Shelter said wryly.

"It's a sure enough human mare," Jack Riley said, his breathing heavy. "With everything that counts beneath that dress."

"She's young," Frank Tyler added.

Then the buckboard was gone and Dent rode up, rain running from his hat brim. The door was unlocked and the men herded in.

There was a new arrangement for sleeping now. One no more comfortable than the other. A length of chain was fastened to an iron ring beside each bare plank bed and they were fastened to these at night.

There was no supper that evening, and night was quick in coming to the dark bunkhouse. They slept restlessly, the rain pattering on the roof of the tight barracks. And each man slept with a part of his mind on the faceless, nameless woman in the buckboard.

It was still raining at dawn, the orange sun bleeding out against the screen of quicksilver. Frank Tyler hunched close to Shell as they drank their morning meal—beef broth and bacon rind. The kid was doing well enough through all of this. He had aged some, his cheeks going hollow, his muscles turning to leather beneath his white, womanish skin.

"I'm coming on your crew," Tyler told him.

"All right. Any reason?"

"To get out of the rain," Frank told him with a quick smile. Shell grinned in return. No matter how rough it got outside, everyone knew the work inside the mine was the most dangerous, the most wearing.

"She's still here," Duncan told them all, helping himself to a second cup of the soapy tasting broth.

"The woman?" Riley asked, his head snapping up. "How do you know?"

"Those bay ponies," Duncan said under his breath. "They're still in the corral." Duncan knew horses and loved them. He had been a breeder, and those horses were more beautiful perhaps to him than the woman who had remained faceless, a beauty in imagination. "I noticed 'em right off."

"Who?" Frank asked. "Who can she be?"

Duncan shrugged. "If she's staying here, she must be something to old man Zukor. Sister, cousin, wife."

"Prob'ly his mother," Riley said sourly.

"What's the damned difference!" Corson put in angrily. They glanced at him and he added, "None of us will ever see a woman up close again."

The rain slanted down, a wind twisting the sheets of water into convoluted gray curtains. The wagon was late, and when it arrived Depew was in a nasty mood.

"I was better off staring at the back end of cows all day," he muttered. "They was about as pretty as you scum anyway."

It was damp in the mine, water seeped through the stone, ponding on the floors, trickling off down the shafts. A third shaft had been built, this one angling sharply down to follow a jagged vein of ore. There was a foot of water in the bottom of it, and here and there red mud oozed from the walls of the shaft.

"I'm damned if I'll go down there," Corson said angrily. "Without shoring, in this wet . . . we're askin' for a cave-in."

"What about Swede and Torres?" Frank Tyler asked. His lean face was splotched with the moving flame of the torch he carried. "Can't they shore it?"

"They told Swede they don't have the timber, can't cut it in this weather, and anyway it wasn't necessary."

"I don't like it," Fox said. The breed was not shy about dangerous work, but this was something none of them had a taste for.

"We don't start hauling some ore out, Dent's going to come looking for us," Corson reminded them bitterly.

"We'll have to make the best of it," Shell said. "Work slow, take it easy." He lowered himself into the shaft, his torch flickering over the walls. Reaching the bottom Shell found himself standing in knee deep water. "It's rising still!" he called up.

They tried bailing, but to no avail. The water was seeping in faster than they could get it out with the buckets. Shell stood, wiping his face. Fox was beside him, the two men having no success.

"Somebody's got to talk to Dent," the breed said finally, with disgust.

"I'll do it," Shelter volunteered. Corson and Tyler gave him a hand up and he scrambled onto the horizontal shaft, soaking wet, mud clinging to him.

"It won't do any good," Corson said miserably.

"Maybe not," Shelter admitted.

Swede was just arriving, pick in hand, warily surveying the dark, damp shaft. His face was painted with fear. The mud was sloughing off into the main shaft, and it took no experience to see they were running the risk of being buried alive.

Shell brushed by him, slapped his back encouragingly and wound toward the mine entrance. Banquero was just inside the shaft, staying out of the rain. He was carrying ore down the ladders and his basket rested beside him. His black eyes flashed toward Shelter who nodded and strode past, going to the ladder himself.

"Hold it there, Morgan!" Depew's voice boomed up from below. Shelter stood, cupping his hands to call above the roar of the rain.

"I want to talk to Dent!"

Depew was bundled in a slicker, the rain streaming off his hat as it blew in in cold sheets from the north. Shell's teeth chattered. Shirtless, soaked to the bone he called out again.

"We have to talk to Dent!"

"What's holding things up?" Depew hollered back angrily.

"The damned shaft's flooding out, we can't go down!"

Angrily the guard turned away, returning a few minutes later with Dent who wore a black slicker, black hat. He waved Shelter down with a gloved hand and Shell climbed down the rickety ladder, making out Duncan and Jack Riley through the screen of iron gray rain. The two big men shivered next to the empty ore crusher.

"What the hell's going on?" Dent demanded.

"We got water in the shaft, without shoring . . ."

"How much water?" Dent wanted to know.

"Two and a half feet right now, but . . ."

"You can work in that," Dent snapped. He started to turn away and Shell put a hand on his shoulder. Instantly he turned and the hickory club fell across Shell's shoulder, stunning Morgan with pain.

"It'll cave in, damn it!" Shell persisted.

"And you'd like to take the day off, have a picnic? I told you, Morgan—you can work in that shaft!"

"Have a look, Dent! Damn it, just come have a look."

Dent's eyes lifted to the cavern above. "No." He turned then and walked away, nodding to the guard.

"That's settled then," Depew said. "Now get your butt back up that ladder and get to work, Morgan."

Shelter stood there helplessly a minute before turning angrily and walking to the ladder, the rain cold across his back, his shoulder flaming with pain. He tested the shoulder, decided it wasn't broken and climbed slowly up the ladder, the wind buffeting his back as the rain washed past.

Banquero sat on his heels, watching Shell with a thin smile of amusement. Shell ignored the Apache and walked into the mine shaft.

Eyes lifted to him as he rounded the bend and walked to the new shaft which was marked by a pile of rubble. Corson shook his head and turned away, not having to ask.

"Well?" Swede was absolutely petrified.

"Dig, the man said," Shell told him tersely. Swede peered into the gaping shaft, listening to the water trickle into the pond far below.

"I can't . . ." Swede said. He spread pleading hands.

"Tex," Shell said to Corson. "It's you and me; Frank, Jim Fox and the Swede will haul for us."

"All right," Corson said sourly. "I'll have a line on me," the Texan said to Tyler. "That mud starts sliding you get me the hell out. Fast."

Shell was also tying a line on, though he doubted it would do much good. That mud would weigh many tons; if it did come loose they were done for. "Maybe the rain'll stop," he said without much expectation of it happening, or doing any real good.

"I'll spell you at noon," Frank Tyler offered. Fox nodded.

"You two go till noon," the breed said, "then the kid and me."

Swede knew he was expected to say something, to make an offer, but the gambler didn't have it in him. He looked away in shame.

"Let's have at it, Tex," Shell said. Taking a deep breath he took two picks and a shovel over his shoulder, moving down cautiously into the dank shaft. Corson followed with a torch, holding an ore bucket.

It was gruelling work. Standing in a cold pond of water at the bottom of the dark shaft they picked at the ore-bearing quartz, breaking it free. Their legs grew numb, their backs knotted. Occasionally the surrounding earth would break loose, great slabs of earth and mud sloughing off into the pool of water, burying the ore, putting out the torches, raising the water level.

Shell's shoulder ached, but he tried to put it out of his mind. There is only one way to endure such work, and that is to make it the entire focus of your mind. He worked methodically, involving his thoughts with nothing but the vein, the strokes of his pick.

A wall of mud broke free and Corson cursed again, standing looking upward, the tendons on his neck taut, his mouth pulled down with grief.

"God damn 'em!" he screamed. "They'll kill me. Kill me for this!" He picked up a fist-sized chunk of quartz, holding it out to Morgan. "Look at what you're dying for!"

Shelter nodded, sagging momentarily against the cold, muddy wall of the shaft. The ore was not that good. Threads of gold could be seen distinctly, but narrow, fine threads. Low-grade ore which could only be profitably mined with cheap labor, by cutting all corners, ignoring safety entirely.

"For this . . ." Corson said in a low voice, and he was shaking as he said it.

"Tex!" Frank Tyler had stripped to the waist. He leaned over the shaft, calling down, "Come on up. I'll take a turn."

Corson turned away from Morgan and glanced up, slowly recovering himself. He nodded and answered. "All right. Thanks, kid!"

Unsteadily Corson climbed out, Frank Tyler appearing in his place moments later. Shell nodded to the kid, "That was big of you."

"It's my turn," Tyler shrugged, picking up a shovel.

"He was cracking," Shell said, "and you know it."

"Maybe."

Together they worked silently, with the constant cold, the only light that cast by the wavering torches. The water continued to rise, the seeping above adding to it constantly.

"How's Swede?" Shell asked the kid.

"Not good. Those drays are too heavy for him. We tried loading him light, but Depew caught on and put a stop to it."

"Still raining out?"

"Still raining."

The going was painfully slow, the hours passing at a walk. Tyler was game for the work, but he didn't have the strength he needed, and he tired easily.

"Slow down," Shell told him.

"They're already complaining about the amount of ore," Tyler told him, and with a half-smile the kid put his back to it, giving it what he had.

He had been thinking of something, it seemed to Shell a couple of times he had caught the kid glancing at him as if he had something to say. Now Tyler came out with it.

"You'd better keep an eye open," Tyler told him.

"Why?" Banquero flashed into Shell's thoughts, but the Apache had seemed subdued lately, and he doubted Banquero would try it again.

"Dent. Zukor. They've got the idea in their heads that one of us is not a prisoner, but some kind of government man."

"That worries them?"

"It does. They can't know what information has gotten out. They're worried . . . and Morgan, I've heard talk, they're sure it's you."

"Me?" Shell shook his head.

"Sure. You're the only man who didn't come down from Steamboat. You kind of invited yourself, you might say."

"They're barking up the wrong tree," Shell said. "It's not me. I'm just plain dumb—that's what put me here."

"I know it," Tyler said, straightening up to look at Shelter Morgan. "I know because it's me, Morgan. I'm the government man."

Shell was silent a moment. Leaning on his shovel he pondered it. "I see," he said, "and those folks you thought would be in contact in Strawberry . . ."

"Federal marshals. We've been trying to get a line on this business with Judge Fainer and Sheriff Chambers."

"Well," Shell replied, "you've got it now."

"Yeah." Frank Tyler nodded, looking around at the flooded shaft. "I've got it now."

They shoveled the ore into the buckets and Shell asked, "Think there's a chance those marshals will find us?"

"Up here?" Tyler shrugged, "I doubt it. The place is a fortress, and they've no idea where to look."

"Well, there's a chance . . . that's somethin' to wish on, at least."

"I wish you wouldn't mention this to anyone

else," Tyler said sincerely. "I told you because I think you might be in danger because of it. I hear you were poking around up here before you were arrested. The other men—I'm one of them now—but their feelings might change if they knew I was the law."

"I'll keep your secret," Shell promised.

Well it was little enough in the way of hope. Before the rain had begun there was a chance, a slim one, that a good Indian tracker could have followed their sign to this mountain. By now the weather would have erased any tracks, however. Still there was a chance—an overheard remark, a chance discovery. Men cling to such slender hopes under circumstances like these.

After noon, Shelter crawled out of the hole, muddy, soaked, chilled. He dragged himself up onto the level and sat shaking his head. Corson was there, watching him grimly, and Fox.

"I guess it's my turn," the half breed said morosely.

"I'll stay down if you like, Jim," Shell offered.

"No. I made my bargain, I'll stick with it."

Frank Tyler clawed his way up, his muddy hand taking Shell's. The kid sagged beside Shelter, muddy from head to foot. "It's getting worse down there," Frank told them.

"It'll be worse all afternoon," Shell told Fox regretfully. "That earth is just getting softer, and it's sliding plenty now."

"I'll go," Fox said slowly. He added a deep curse under his breath as he peered into the shaft. Shell had risen and was drying off on his shirt which had been left above. Ruefully he studied his boots and trousers.

"Damn these irons," Shell cursed, "I'd give a lot to be able to get these pants off."

Swede arrived, dragging an empty sledge. His face was white, drawn. He blinked at Shelter and then at Corson who was stripping off his shirt again, preparing to join Fox in the shaft.

"Let me go," Swede said miserably and Corson's head snapped around in surprise.

"You don't want to go down there," Tex Corson told the gambler.

"I can't go on with this," Swede panted. "This sledge—it's too much for me. My heart's going to give out." He looked pleadingly from Corson to Shelter and back. "Please!"

"You don't have the picture quite right, Swede," Morgan said gently. "The shaft—that's plain hazardous right now."

"I'll never make another round with the sledge," Swede insisted. "Tex! Please!"

"Hell," Corson said, "you're welcome to it if you think you can cut that better." He waved a disgusted hand at the pit.

"Fine," Swede breathed.

"You can't, Swede." Shelter put a hand on the gambler's shoulder. "That's a bitch down there, boy." Swede hesitated. "I'll help you with your sledge."

"I want to work in the shaft!" Angrily the Swede slapped Shelter's hand away. "That crawling . . . my knees are rubbed to the bone. My hands . . ." he held out two bloody hunks of meat with fingers on them.

"Listen . . ." Shell began, but Swede shot back,

"Damnit! Who put you in charge, Morgan? It's all right with Tex, and I want to trade off! Damnit, butt out!"

Corson shrugged and Shelter stepped away. Swede hefted a shovel and a pick and slowly lowered himself to the shaft floor. Corson picked up Swede's sledge and loaded it. Frank and Shell settled in to drawing the ore up.

The cold rain still fell outside, and the wind twisted through the tunnel, chilling Shelter who was soaked right through. Hand over hand he hauled the ore out, dumped the rocks onto the waiting sledge — Banquero's or Corson's, lowered the bucket and waited. It was growing darker, Shell saw with relief. Within the hour they would have to quit. God, that bare bunkhouse sounded good just then.

It was warm, dry at least, and . . . Shell's head snapped up. There was a hollow rumbling, a trickle of water where none had been before. Then the wall gave way, and the shaft was buried under tons of muddy earth.

"God damn!" Tyler leaped away, startled, but Shelter was already moving forward, toward the pit where still more mud was sloughing off. He pulled hard on the lifeline, feeling an incredible weight against him.

"Get on this line," he shouted to Tyler who staggered forward, taking the rope behind Shell. "Banquero! Corson!" Shell hollered up the tunnel, but he saw no one. Desperately they tugged on the rope and after a long minute the line moved.

There was heavy suction on the line, drawing the weight downward, but they managed to raise it an inch at a time.

"There!" Shell nodded and pulled again, harder. Corson was coming on the run, Banquero behind him.

Shell's eyes were fixed on the line. There was a mud-daubed hand clinging to the line, and they pulled again, desperately. Slowly the arm emerged and they pulled the man out.

Jim Fox, strangling on the mud which clogged his nostrils, eyes, mouth. They turned him on his side, and Shelter dug the mud from Fox's mouth with his fingers, flushing it with the canteen water which Corson brought.

Gagging, choking Fox rolled slowly over and got to a seated posture, looking at the men crouched around him as if he were seeing ghosts.

"Close one," he panted. "Real close."

Of Swede they said nothing. He had not been clinging to the lifeline. It would take most of two days to dig that mud from the pit. Shelter stood on wobbly legs and stared into the flooded shaft.

"That's four," Shelter said to himself. Banquero glanced up. "Four of us they've killed. Who's next?"

10.

Outside the storm raged. Silver rain drummed down from jumbled black clouds, pelting the dark earth. Now and again brilliant bursts of white chain lightning illuminated the black world outside, and the thunder guns boomed in the long canyons.

The wind twisted through the timber on the high bluffs and swayed the huge oaks outside Hamilton Zukor's parlor window. He stood before the window a long while, watching the wind and the rain. Then with a sigh, Zukor turned back toward the fireplace where a cedar log burned.

He sensed rather than saw or heard the girl on the staircase, and his milky eyes went to Sylvia who stood on the landing, clutching the green silk wrapper she wore around her throat. Sylvia was a pretty thing, Zukor decided, pleasant company. But his wife's niece had chosen the worst of all possible times to come west. Zukor forced a smile to form on his thick lips.

"The storm wake you, dear?" he asked his niece.

"Yes." Sylvia nodded and hesitantly came down into the parlor. The firelight glossed her abundant dark hair, and lent her fine features a warm glow. She wore a necklace with a single, perfect pearl. It had settled in the hollow of her throat and Zukor's eyes fixed on it, fascinated.

"I find the rain somewhat relaxing myself," Hamilton Zukor said. He walked to the liquor cabinet and poured a snifter of brandy. Sylvia watched the light play in the amber liquid, illuminate her uncle's heavy features.

"It's not only the rain," Sylvia explained. "I'm uncomfortable here. You were right, I should have stayed down at the ranch."

Zukor nodded amiably; thank God the girl was uncomfortable, wanted to leave. "As soon as the rain stops, I'll see that a buckboard is made available."

"Good." Sylvia leaned back in the red velvet chair and sighed audibly. "I don't know how you can stand it either, Uncle. These convicts . . . it frightens me to think of it. Then too, I feel a twinge of sorrow for them . . . they seem utterly miserable, brutalized. They're little more than animals, actually."

"Exactly!" Zukor exclaimed. "They are hard, dangerous men. If I could relate what some of them have done . . . I wouldn't wish to frighten you more. Yet I have done them a tremendous favor, and I believe helped myself some little bit."

Sylvia's eyes narrowed, wishing to believe, not quite finding belief in her heart. Zukor took another long drink and stood with his back to the crackling fire, rocking on his heels.

"Not a man among them would be alive today if I had not arranged to have them on my work gangs, Sylvia. They would have been hung from the nearest tree, their lives ended without having produced a single ounce of good for themselves or anyone else. Here they are fed, they breathe fresh air. They live," Zukor congratulated himself.

"If that is life."

"A prisoner's life," Zukor shrugged. He refilled his glass from the cut crystal decanter. "And there are several men I believe may eventually be rehabilitated," he lied. "If they keep their noses clean, do their work, I plan to eventually shift them to lighter duties, removing their chains as they prove progressively trustworthy." He moved nearer to the girl.

"Dear Sylvia, do not think me a beast because I must be their warden — I am giving them a chance when society has said they shall have no more chances."

His hand dropped to Sylvia's shoulder and she

withdrew from it slightly, finding it chilly, wooden. She leaned her head back and smiled as if accepting it all. Yet the cold light in Hamilton Zukor's eyes told another story. She wanted to be away from here.

Zukor went again to the window, seeing a spectacular burst of lightning brighten the red hills. When he turned back again, Sylvia had disappeared. He heard her bedroom door shut moments later and he smiled grimly, cursing his foolish wife for allowing the girl on the mountain.

His glass again was empty and Zukor had turned toward the sideboard when he heard the rapping at the front door. He frowned and crossed the room. Who, at this hour?

Zukor opened the door a crack and the wind drove a few drops of cold rain into the room. Wes Chambers stood there, rain slick, his face glossed coldly by the rain.

"Sheriff?" Zukor glanced at the big clock on the wall behind him then reluctantly let Wes Chambers in. The sheriff removed his slicker and hat, rolling up the sleeves of the red flannel shirt he wore underneath.

"I'd like to talk to you privately," Chambers said.

"All right," Zukor said unhappily. He was ready to turn in, looking forward to a few minutes before the fire, a last nightcap. He led Chambers into his office which was still not completed. His desk sat squarely in the center of the room, crates of books and furnishings clustered around it.

"What is it?" Zukor settled heavily into his chair, studying the dark eyed deputy, not liking the slightly mocking expression on Chambers' craggy face.

"I've been talking to Dent," Chambers said, leaning forward in his chair, hands clasped. "There's a story going around among the prisoners and the guards have picked up on it."

"What kind of story?" Zukor asked impatiently.

Chambers tilted back, putting his hands together behind his neck. "There's a government man in camp," he said slowly, enjoying the effect.

"A government man!" Zukor went crimson then white, drumming his fingers on the desk top. "But it's only a story," Zukor shrugged. Chamber's smile had not changed.

"No. I don't think so. I think it's true, and I believe we've identified the man."

"Who?"

"Shelter Morgan." Chambers had to explain, "The tall blond man."

"Tell me all about it," Zukor said, sighing again. The fat man leaned back, watching Chambers who related it all with perverse relish.

"Seems that Shelter Morgan was poking around up here before the new batch of prisoners arrived. Sam Yawkey stopped him at the lower guard point. He had the Dolittle girl with him, but apparently he was only using her to get him past Yawkey and to show him the mountains."

"The girl doesn't . . ."

"I've talked to her." Chambers lifted a hand. "She doesn't know anything. She talks freely about Morgan, which is unlikely for a government investigator. Besides," he shrugged, "she's only a kid."

"I can't see how you've drawn your conclusions."

"Listen and you will," Chambers said sharply. Zukor's mouth tightened, but he nodded.

"Go ahead."

"When I brought down this gang from Steamboat who did we find on the trail but Morgan?"

"Coincidence?"

"Sure," Chambers smiled. "What do you suppose happens next?" Wes picked up a pencil and began playing with it. He lifted his eyes to Zukor who was watching back impatiently.

"You tell me."

"I intend to. Three men show up in Strawberry not a week after delivery. All wearing broadcloth suits, white shirts. Supposed to be railroad men or some such, but Luke poked around in their hotel room. What do you suppose he found?"

"I couldn't say."

"United States Marshals' documents, Mister Zukor."

"What did they want to know?"

"What do you think?" Chambers smiled thinly. "They never talked to me, of course, but they asked around town—folks talk. Wanted to know about some prisoners. Wanted to know a lot of things . . . but they didn't learn a thing."

"I see." Zukor stood and crossed the room worriedly. All of this had been built on the premise that no one would know or care what had happened to prisoners sentenced to death. That it would be impossible for the convict labor to be traced. Now it seemed not so impossible. And if they found out . . . men had died here; men were being illegally imprisoned. "If any information gets out, we're done," Zukor said, and he was sweating. "Morgan must be taken care of."

"That's exactly what I was thinking, Mister Zukor," Wes Chambers said with slow satisfaction. Zukor had the feeling Chambers was holding something back, but that did not strike him as important just now.

What was important was getting rid of Shelter Morgan. But how? If any information had gotten out, if those marshals happened on the mine and its workers, the last thing Zukor wanted was the murder of a U.S. marshal on his hands.

"Have you got any ideas?" he asked Chambers.

The sheriff nodded slowly, his face a mask of pleasure. "I've an idea. Now you tell me what you think of it."

"Knowing you, you probably want to put a bullet in his head," Zukor said heavily.

"Nothing would please me more," Chambers said with a savagery which startled even Zukor. "But it won't work out. Nor would an accident of any kind—we'd still be to blame for that, wouldn't we? And I'm not taking the penalty for killing a Federal marshal."

"Then what?"

"I'll tell you. Up to this point we're legal. Maybe Judge Fainer is bending the law, but that's his lookout. I've got the legal documents, and I've got them locked up in my safe which prove Fainer remanded those prisoners to my custody. And there's nothing new or illegal about me hiring those prisoners out as a work gang. We're clear so far, at least as to any major crimes.

"I mean to keep it that way," Wes Chambers said. "There's a killing that needs to be done, but we don't do it."

"Who then?"

"Who do you think? One thing we've got plenty of is killers out there." Chambers smiled.

"The men!"

"That's right. The convicts. If this marshal is found out and the prisoners do him in—well, that's his tough luck for getting himself into it, isn't it? We can't protect him if we didn't even know who he was."

"How do the men feel about Morgan now?"

"They like him," Chambers acknowledged. "So Dent says. He's one of their leaders."

"Then . . ."

"Don't you worry, Mister Zukor. They may like him now, but by the time we're finished, they'll be ready to tear him limb from limb. There won't be a man out there who won't give everything he has, ever had, or will have to kill Shelter Morgan!"

"*Now* you have something that sounds interesting," Hamilton Zukor said, leaning back in his leather chair. "Tell me all about it."

The mine wagon rolled through the morning mists. The sun was a pale, iron-gray promise in the eastern sky. The men stood before the barracks, shivering. Their stomachs were empty, their muscles stiff with the hard labor and cold nights. Torres had a nasty cough which sawed through the morning periodically. Duncan stamped his feet vigorously, the breath steaming from his lips as he tried desperately to keep warm.

In the middle of the night the cold rain had turned to snow. The wind was unabating. Depew stepped from the wagon box and stood at a distance, his rifle levelled.

"Load it up," he ordered.

Obediently they marched forward through the thick red mud, chains clanking. Duncan climbed up, then Jack Riley, breathing a curse. Shelter started to follow, but Depew waved him aside.

"Not you, Morgan! Not this morning."

Shelter shrugged, glanced at Frank Tyler and at Corson who was mystified, then stepped back, letting Banquero and Torres clamber aboard the wagon.

The driver snapped his whip and turned the team, the guards following as the mine wagon rolled up the narrow trail through the gray mist. Depew stood waiting, watching Shelter. When the wagon was gone he took two steps forward.

"What's up?" Shell asked cautiously.

"Looks like your star's rising," Depew answered. "Mister Zukor needs a stable hand, a man to see to the horses. You've been elected."

"Why me?" Shell asked skeptically. "Duncan knows horses."

"Duncan has murdered six men," Depew replied roughly. "How about you, Morgan? Are you a murderer?"

"No," he answered. "No, I'm not."

"All right. There's a reason. Don't fight your luck, Morgan. You know what this means, don't you?"

"What does it mean?" Shell repeated.

"Them." Depew nodded at Shell's irons. "You'll have those irons struck off your ankles."

"Off?" the idea was incredible just then. Shelter looked at Depew through the falling mist. Those leg irons had become a part of him. His gait had become adjusted to their ungainly weight. The rawness in his ankles he had become accustomed to. Off! He nodded to Depew. "Anything."

"You see you hold your end up, Morgan," Depew said. "And don't get the idea this means you can make a run. It's the man without chains you watch closest."

Shell nodded agreeably although they both knew that was the first thing that came into Shelter's mind—making a run. It was the all-dominating thought of any bound man. But for now . . . they moved toward the stables across the pasture. Shell walked stiffly, Depew followed on his Appaloosa.

It was a good quarter of a mile through the rain and shifting low clouds. The grass was unnaturally bright in this gray light, the air incredibly fresh. The stable lay ahead, a gray, low building with a peaked roof and a collection of barked cottonwood-log corrals attached. A wagon with a load of baled hay, covered with a canvas tarp, sat to one side.

With Depew still mounted and following him, Shelter opened the high door to the barn, glad to be out of the rain. There were a dozen or so work horses which were used to draw the mine wagons, and some saddle stock in the stalls. A cursory glance told Shelter there was plenty of work to be done.

All of the horses wore a heavy, uncurried winter coat. A bay gelding stood uncomfortably as if it was having trouble with its hock. At any rate, Shelter found by lifting the foreleg of several of the horses, they all were sadly in need of shoes.

A cobweb-strung forge sat in one corner, and blacksmith's tools hung on pegs from the wall.

"We had a smith for a couple of weeks," Depew said, "a man named Tankers. He up and quit, said he didn't favor the place."

"Can't understand that," Shell said.

"His quarters are through that door," Depew motioned with his rifle. "There's no windows, no outside door. But it's bound to be more comfortable than where you been sleeping."

"You mean I'll be staying here," Shell asked with surprise, "not in the barracks?"

"That's it," Depew told him. "As long as you watch your step. You've fallen into luck, Morgan. Don't abuse it. You can be put back in that mine if you prefer it."

"What about these?" Shell nodded down at the leg irons he wore.

"You got the tools, don't you?" Depew asked. Then the guard turned his pony and walked it toward the door. He stopped and without turning back said in a low, flat voice, "You make a run, Morgan, and we'll shoot you down like a dog."

Depew rode out into the rain, the door fluttering in the wind behind him. Shell crossed to the door and shut it. He was puzzled, deeply puzzled.

He looked at the irons on his legs and went to the forge, firing it up. Was this what they wanted? Was

130

it some sort of trap? Let him run, then shoot him? Why, when they already had him?

Maybe what Depew had said was the truth. Maybe Zukor had decided that Shelter was not so dangerous as some of the others—he needed a stablehand, that was obvious. The truth? Shell shook his head; he had reservations.

But the chains would come off. No matter what was to follow, the chains would come off. With a file he took off the flared heads of the locking pins, then drove the pins through with a hammer and punch. The irons fell away and Shell stood staring at them. Links of cold iron against the stable floor. His ankles were ugly beneath them. Bruised, torn open, raw to the bone in front.

Shelter went to the bellows, forcing the air into the forge which was already glowing. Then he lifted the chains with tongs and placed them inside the forge. When the irons had begun to glow a cherry red, Morgan pulled them out, and with a hammer he beat the ankle irons to a shapeless mass, the golden sparks flying as he destroyed the symbols of slavery.

He worked angrily, his hammer driving against the anvil until the sweat poured from his forehead. Then, satisfied, he held the ankle irons up with the tongs.

"I'm not sure I like them," he heard a voice say. He turned, a curse on his lips, to see the beautiful young woman standing in the doorway, a riding hood on her head. "That seems a lot of work for nothing," Sylvia said, coming a step nearer.

"It wasn't for nothing," Shell muttered. Slowly

he lowered the misshapen irons into an iron bucket filled with water, the steam hissing fiercely as the metal cooled. Shell turned them over, watching as the water stopped boiling, as the iron went cold. Then he pulled them up and threw them on the earth. "No other man will wear those," he told the girl with a grim smile.

"Then you have accomplished something," Sylvia said. She lowered her hood and her abundant dark hair, jeweled with scattered raindrops fell across her shoulders.

"Who are you?" Shell asked.

"Sylvia Woods," she replied. "I wanted to go riding so I came to saddle my horse. The roan with the three white stockings," she nodded.

"Riding on a day like this?"

"I have to get out of the house," Sylvia said. "Off this place." She smiled then, a full smile which delighted Shelter. There was a coy enticement in her dark eyes, he thought. Suddenly the girl stopped smiling. Her eyes which had been sweeping Shell's long frame had found his ankles.

"My God!" she exclaimed. Her hand went to her mouth. "You're one of . . . them."

"A prisoner? Yes."

"You're escaping . . . and I'm talking to you like a ninny."

"I'm not escaping," Shell said. "And you needn't look at me like that. I'm no butcher, and I don't hurt little girls."

"But you're here," she argued. "I was told that all of you . . ."

"Not me," Shelter said severely. He turned and

132

went to the wooden barrel where the iron stock was kept, finding what he needed for the new horse-shoes.

Sylvia watched the blond man, liking the way he moved, the muscles which corrugated his shoulders and bare chest when he worked. "Will you saddle my horse?" she asked.

"If that's part of my job," Shell said. She was standing near to him now, so near that he could smell the soap and jasmine powder she had dusted with.

"Don't you know," Sylvia asked, "what your job is?"

"My first day," Shell shrugged. He did not smile as he spoke, despite the wrinkles Sylvia detected around his blue-gray eyes, wrinkles caused by frequent, deep laughter. "Look—" Shell's eyes went to the door. "I'll saddle your horse if you like, but you'd better get on out of here. I'm sure Zukor wouldn't like it much. And they don't need much of an excuse to come down hard on me."

"My uncle . . .!" Sylvia began. Then suddenly she decided she would prefer not to mention that she was related to Hamilton Zukor. This man, after all, was one of his convicts. "My uncle used to say that a lady needs to learn discretion if one is to continue to be regarded as a lady. Saddle my roan, if you will, and I'll leave rapidly, discretely."

"It's best." Shell had already swung her side-saddle from the stall and he was smoothing the blanket on the roan's back. He rubbed the bit in his hands for a moment before slipping it into the roan's mouth. All of it, every movement, was done with a deft sureness which Sylvia's eyes caught. Hard-muscled, smooth, this stablehand was all man, sure in his physical capabilities.

She took his strong hand and got onto the saddle, letting her fingers linger a little longer than necessary on his. Thanking him, she slipped out into the mist-obscured day, her heart racing as she let the roan find an easy canter.

She had wanted nothing more than to leave this dismal mountain, threatening bleak place it was. Now Sylvia was not so sure. It had become suddenly exciting, and she rode through the rain-screened countryside concentrating her thoughts on the tall blond stablehand with those magnificent shoulders.

11.

The sky had cleared briefly at mid-morning, but by noon a new storm had settled in, chilling the miners as they gathered around the stew pot for a tasteless lunch they spooned down rapidly for the warmth. Jack Riley walked with his plate back to the ore crusher. There he could be out of the rain beneath an overhanging eave.

Morosely the big man stared into the distances, cursing all of nature and all of mankind. He picked up a movement out of the corner of his eye and glanced up, finding Dent there.

"How's the slop?" the guard said.

"How do you think?" Jack Riley answered with a growl.

"Tough," Dent shrugged. He stood, hands behind his back, the rain falling all around. "What I get ain't much better," Dent said. There was no response from Riley, so he went on.

"I'd give a lot to be out of this rain. But they give the new men the soft jobs."

Jack Riley pushed his plate aside and sat glaring at Dent, not giving a damn about the guards' problems.

"I was here six months before Morgan," Dent said. At that Jack Riley perked up. His eyes opened wide with curiosity and Dent smiled to himself. "Time to get with it, Riley," Dent said suddenly, glancing at his watch.

"What did you mean about Morgan?" Jack Riley struggled to his feet. Dent shrugged.

"It's obvious, isn't it?" At Jack Riley's confused frown, Dent added, "Hell, man! Don't tell me you haven't figured it out yet? Are you that slow?"

Jack Riley didn't like the insinuation. He had always been called dumb, slow-witted, thick-headed. He had killed a man for saying it once, but he was curious. "I don't get it, no," he told Dent.

"Why, Morgan was working with us," Dent said casually. "Keeping an eye on you boys, an ear open to any escape talk."

"You're a damned liar!" Riley exploded.

Dent turned icy eyes on Riley, and his hickory stick came into Riley's view. The guard said in a low voice, "How the hell you think he got cut loose? He asked out, couldn't cut the work no more."

"Shelter Morgan?"

"That's right. Think he just wandered in and joined this gang because he took a liking to you boys?"

"You roughed him up pretty good."

"Had to. It had to look good." Dent shook his head. "Boy, he *was* good at his job, keeping you fooled like this."

"Morgan . . ." Riley shook his bearded, buffalo's head in confusion.

"By now he's got those chains off, he's dry and dining on steak and taters."

"I can't believe it," Riley said.

"Don't!" Dent shrugged. "Just ask yourself where is he? And next time you meet up, don't forget to say 'boss' to Shelter Morgan."

Again Dent looked at his watch. Duncan was returning through the rain to join Riley at the ore crusher. "Get with it, Riley," Dent said, "lunch is over."

Duncan plodded up, leaning against the handle on the huge spindle. Dent had walked off, but Riley still had not taken up his position opposite Duncan.

"What's up?" Duncan wanted to know, and Riley told him.

"Can you beat that," Duncan responded, shaking his head. "You believe it?"

"I don't know," Riley shrugged. "What would Dent lie for? Where the hell is Morgan, anyway?"

Slowly the two men put their weight to the

spindle handles, moving the jaws of the ore crusher downward. Duncan spoke again without looking up.

"Fits what I heard," the giant said.

"What's that?"

"That there was some kind of government man here. They say he was only making sure things were legal here."

"Morgan?"

"I dunno," Duncan shrugged. "It's just what they say."

"Then maybe we're in luck," Riley brightened up.

"How do you figure?"

"This can't be legal," Riley replied. "Slaves is what we are."

"I dunno. A judge sent us here, a sheriff delivered us. I heard tell of plenty of work gangs. I figure as long as they feed us, give us shelter, it's all legal."

"That's what Morgan would report?"

"I dunno that it's Morgan," Duncan muttered. "I don't know that Morgan's *anything*. Hell, they could have taken him off and blown his brains out."

"Yeah, that's right," Jack Riley agreed. "We don't know what happened to Morgan. I wouldn't believe nothin' that son of a bitch, Dent tells me."

Riley put his bulk to the handle of the ore crusher, walking in an endless circle through the pouring rain. He was far from convinced after talking to Duncan who had a cooler head . . . still, a man had to wonder. He had the rest of the day to worry the notion.

Shelter had done a good day's work. Four sets of shoes and a mended bridle, a haircut for the buckskin which he favored for its deep chest and stocky legs. It looked to be a long-riding horse, and that was what Shell had in mind.

Whatever they had in mind for him, he had no intention of staying long enough to find out. They had all of the passes guarded or blocked, but Shelter would have his try. There was too much at stake. It was Chambers' hide he wanted.

First he had to shed the irons. That was done. Now they had given him access to a horse. With a gun, Shelter would take his chance if the chance presented itself.

He stood in the doorway, mopping his face as the sunset flashed on the high clouds. Down the long trail from the mine he could see the wagons rolling in, and he stood a minute longer, watching.

The first face he recognized was that of Jack Riley. The big man's head came around and he stared at Shelter, hard. There was no friendliness in that look. Riley was beside Frank Tyler and he punched Tyler.

Frank's head swiveled as well and Shell lifted a hand. Tyler waved back. Big Jack Riley did not. Banquero sat on the tail gate, his leg irons dangling, black eyes on Shelter Morgan.

Shelter stood looking after them a moment, then the wagons swung away toward the barracks. Darkness was closing in, the last silver gleaming of daylight edging the clouds above the northern mountains. Shelter turned back into the stable, walking to the small room which had been assigned to him.

There was a tick mattress on a roughly framed bed, a chair and a hook on the wall to hang your coat and pants. Shell lay back on the bed in the cool darkness, his mind sorting through the problem once again.

There had to be a man posted outside, watching the barracks and the stable. Where was he? Was there more than one? The nearest cover was a good two hundred yards off, too far even on a good horse. Yet in the stormy weather, the night . . . Shell's head lifted slowly.

There was someone else in the stable.

Cautiously he swung his feet to the floor and moved to the door. In passing he wrapped his hand around the handle of a pitchfork.

It was dark in the stable, smelling of horses and hay. A ribbon of faint gray light seeped through the main door—a door which had been tightly latched a moment ago. Shell crept forward, keeping to the walls where the shadow was deepest.

Shell stopped, listening to the wind in the eaves, the rain on the roof. He saw nothing, heard nothing but the natural sounds. A rat scuttled across the floor and he flinched, gripping the pitchfork tighter. Silently Shell moved across the stable, pausing next to the buckskin's stall. The horse looked up to Shell, nuzzling his shoulder.

Something moved.

The sound had come from overhead and Shelter's head went up. It came again, a small indefinite sound in the loft and he moved slowly toward the ladder, every sense alert, his steps soft.

Cautiously he gripped the ladder rail and stepped up, pitchfork in his other hand. He eased upward, peering into the loft where five tons of dry hay were stacked against winter. It was pitch black, still as Shell pulled himself up.

A whispered word caused him to spin, raising the pitchfork, as he turned.

"You've got the wrong tool for the job," Sylvia said.

She lay there smiling to him, lying naked in the hay. Shelter slowly lowered the pitchfork, devouring her lush body with his eyes.

"Are you crazy?" he asked.

"Sure." She stretched out a hand to Shelter, beckoning him.

"If Zukor caught us . . ."

"He's gone," Sylvia said. "Gone to Strawberry on business. There's no one around. I slipped past the guards. They're staying out of the rain, and they won't want to come out in it for nothing."

"There's always a chance," Shelter told her.

"Sure there is. I like the danger," Sylvia said. Her lips were parted, her full white breasts inviting. She watched as Shelter slowly put the pitchfork aside then dropped his trousers.

"You like the danger too," Sylvia purred. Her eyes rushed across his flat, hard chest, his heavily muscled thighs, lighting with anticipation at the huge erection he displayed. He came nearer, smiling himself now.

"No. It ain't the *danger* I like," he answered. He

settled beside her on the loose hay and Sylvia's mouth, open, wet, met his passionately.

Drawing her head to him Shell returned the kiss, feeling her probing tongue flicker into his mouth, the soft flesh of her breasts pressed against him.

His hands slid down her smooth back, finding the soft curve of her buttocks, an exploring finger slipping into the warmth between them, bringing a chill of delight to Sylvia's kiss.

She fell away from him, her head lolling back and Shell's lips went to her breasts, finding them full, eager, smelling faintly of the jasmine powder. Sylvia ran her fingers through his hair, holding his head as he searched first one nipple, then the other, finding them taut, and he bit at them hungrily.

"You're kind of rough," Sylvia whispered into his ear.

"Don't you like it?"

"It wasn't a complaint," she answered. She found Shelter's hand resting on her thigh and she interlaced their fingers, taking his hand between her legs where the soft flesh waited beneath the downy hair.

"That's nice," Shell breathed into her ear. She kept her hand pressed over his as his fingers slipped inside, finding her moist, warm. Her knees lifted slightly and she moaned, lifting her mouth to bite at Shell's shoulders, his neck.

"That's nice," Sylvia replied. Her hands had found Shelter's erection, and her fingers ran along the long shaft, going to the head where her thumb traced a series of inflaming patterns. "That's nice."

Her words were moist in his ear, her breath coming in tiny gasps as both her hands explored him, going between his legs, then up along the full erection, feeling the pulse which continued to build.

They lay close together in the hay, the rain drumming a muted rhythm against the roof. Sylvia drew nearer, one of her hands helping Shelter spread her as the other guided him home. For a moment Sylvia let her fingers enjoy their warm flesh, her fingers touching first herself, then Shell's cock before, with an animal gasp she clenched him and drew him all the way in to her demanding depths.

Shell slipped his hands beneath her, gripping her strong, smooth buttocks, and he turned her flat on her back, wanting to drive it all the way home. Sylvia spread her legs, lifting her knees higher as Shell arched his back, then lowered himself, moving in long, tantalizing circles against her. She stretched out eager hands and took his hard buttocks, pulling him to her, tearing at his flesh as he plunged home then withdrew, pausing maddeningly at the very entrance.

"Keep it in," Sylvia begged. "All the way in . . . it's so good." She pulled him wildly to her, her feet lifting into the air, locking behind Shell's back as she rocked in the hay, her head rolling from side to side.

"It's all right, baby," Shell whispered. "Do it. Let go."

Sylvia's body was glossed with perspiration now as she worked her hips against Shell, her pelvis grinding, her abdomen slapping against Shelter's hard belly as she moved still faster, her body sucking at his, working toward an avalanche of feeling.

Suddenly she stopped. Her eyes were half open in the faint light. She ground her teeth together as she swayed against Shell with tiny, measured strokes, finding the exact spot she wanted.

"Now," Shell whispered.

"Yes." She clutched at his shoulder, kissing his cheeks, his chest. Her hands ran down his abdomen to where he entered her and she frantically grabbed at him. "Now," she repeated in a distant voice and Shell felt her burst. Wildly she shook for a moment then was utterly still, taking Shell's head, drawing it to her breasts, petting his hair.

They lay still for a moment. Sylvia's heart beating in Shell's ear. He could feel a matching pulse within her, and he could hold back no longer.

Slowly he began moving against her, his lips going from breast to breast. Sylvia cupped her own breasts, holding them to him as he suckled. Then he kissed her throat, pressing his body against her full length, feeling the rising tension in his loins, the answering throbbing deep within her.

Her juices were on her thighs, on his, and the feel of it, the smell, the nibbling kisses she lavished on his chest as her hands clenched his buttocks, begging for more, brought Shelter off in a driving, plunging climax.

He rocked against her, lifting her legs higher as he reached for her depths, his own pulse pounding in his ears, his legs trembling as his climax flared up, exploded and drained him, Sylvia's warm sighs in his ears, her hungry lips soft against his.

"My God," Sylvia breathed. She sat up as did Shelter, listening to the constant rain on the roof. Her hand stretched out and went between his legs, fondling him, feeling her own juices on him. "I thought I'd had sex before," Sylvia said, nipping at his shoulder.

"You kind of acted like you had," Shell said, kissing the nape of her neck where the soft dark hair fell.

"I've tried," she answered. "But this is the first time I've succeeded . . . like that."

Shelter was silent for a time. He was aware of the coolness of the evening, but warmed by the body of Sylvia pressed against him, her hands between his legs which carefully, minutely explored him.

"Can you ride out of here?" Shelter asked abruptly.

"Right now? With you?" She smiled. "Anywhere. Anytime."

"Not with me. Not right now," Shell answered, his fingers playing with her hair, finding her tiny ear. "Anytime you want to, I mean?"

"Of course! I'm hardly a convict."

"Then you could take a letter out for me."

"A letter—to a girl, I'd bet," Sylvia said. Her lips touched Shell's chest, and her fingers thrilled to the returning erection she felt between his legs.

"A girl, yes. Not a woman, Sylvia."

"Am I a woman, Shell?" she asked, leaning near.

"Far as I can tell," he answered.

"But you're serious about the letter. If I should be found out, it wouldn't be very pleasant."

"They would hurt you?" Shell asked, astonished.

Sylvia thought about that. "No, I don't think so . . . of course I would do it for you."

"It could get me out of here," Shell told her seriously. "I wouldn't want anyone to know." He held her by the shoulders, his eyes searching hers. "They'd kill me, Sylvia."

"I could do that for you. And I swear I wouldn't tell. If I care about anyone on this mountain," she said, leaning her head to his chest so that her soft hair fell across his abdomen and thighs, "it's only for you. This is just a place I had to come to—my father ran off. Mom died."

"I'm sorry," Shell said. Sylvia's head lifted, her lips parted.

"I'm not. Not just now, I'm not one bit sorry."

Her lips went to Shelter's once again, lightly at first, but when he kissed her back, her body tensed and her mouth opened wider.

She fell back against the straw and Shell covered her with his body, his hands running across her hips, between her buttocks and thighs. Her face was flushed, her skin warm despite the chill in the stable and her muscles, beneath the skin rippled with pleasure as his hands stroked her.

"Here." Sylvia rolled away from him and got to her hands and knees. "Like this, once—from behind," she begged.

"Sure."

She waited for him, her muscles twitching in anticipation. Her head was bowed, her long hair trailing into the straw. Shell ran a hand across her pendulous breasts before scooting up behind her, mounting her like a stud stallion.

"Don't wait . . . I can't," Sylvia told him. She shuddered as he eased in behind the soft white moon of her hips, running a hand across them, feeling the silk of her flesh.

"Shelter." She moaned his name, and her hand stretched back, finding him. She centered his erection in her cleft and lifted her head, clenching her teeth with utter joy as he moved into her, driving deeply. "Oh, God," Sylvia said, "now I can feel it there. And there. Harder!" She groaned with immense satisfaction as Shelter moved in still closer, his pelvis against her buttocks, his erection still growing as he felt himself encased in her soft, fluid filled depths.

Again Sylvia's head dropped, and she peered back from between her legs. "I wish I could see, I wish it were light." She breathed heavily through her words, her hand going again and again to where Shelter drove into her, bringing her to a hot, brilliant climax which set off the lights in her head and caused her trembling thighs to go rubbery as he slammed it home again and again, reaching his own shooting climax.

Sylvia lay flat on her belly, her legs spread widely, feeling Shelter's weight against her back, his thick shaft pulsing inside of her as a second wave of rippling warmth rolled over her.

Shell bit her neck lightly, smelling her hair, the lingering scent of her. Sylvia stirred, rolled over and Shell fell out. Quickly she reinserted him, lying there, breathing quietly as the rain continued its constant patter against the roof, as the distant muffled thunder roared up the long canyons.

Later, hurriedly, Shell scratched out a letter to Penny Dolittle. He hated to involve her in this, it was chancy, but he knew no one else. No one within reach.

He pressed the note into Sylvia's hand and she pressed her full lips to his as they parted at the stable door, Sylvia rushing off through the night, the storm.

Shelter watched her go, a faint smile playing on his lips, then he glanced around carefully, seeing no one. He pulled the door shut and bolted it, going to the small room in the rear of the barn, a pleasant weariness upon him.

Carl McGuffie, the guard who had night duty, was sleeping comfortably inside the Zukor porch, and he was aware of nothing except that awakening sleepily, he thought he had heard the sound of a door closing upstairs. Yawning he walked to the curtained porch window and peered into the darkness. Seeing nothing, McGuffie settled again into his chair and drifted off to sleep once more.

The other guards slept in their quarters, but for Depew who had drawn the barracks duty. He awoke each time a convict clanked his leg irons, but that sound in itself was reassuring and he never bothered to rise that night, but once.

Only one pair of eyes had seen the shadowy figure of the woman slipping through the darkness, seen the bare-chested blond man standing in the stable door looking first to the left and then the right before closing the gray door silently behind him.

Depew had let Jack Riley hobble across the way

to the outhouse without bothering to watch him, only counting the minutes to assure himself Riley was within the five-minute rule.

Finishing up, Riley had stepped into the cold rain, black eyes staring across the yard toward the stable. There had been a sound, a shadowy movement, and Jack Riley had frozen in his tracks, watching.

The girl raced back to the Zukor house through the drizzle. Morgan had looked around and then vanished into the stable. Jack Riley had stood still in the darkness for a long minute, his pulse rising to a thudding hammering. He had tried not to believe it about Morgan—he had honestly liked Shelter. Duncan had damned near convinced him that Morgan was not what it was rumored: traitor, spy, lawman.

Now he had news for Duncan, and a rising, crimson anger in his heart. Jack Riley turned, sloshing through the mud toward the open door to the barracks, Depew silently watching him.

12.

The rain had been falling steadily for most of a week, but overnight it turned into a rip-roaring gale. Thunder exploded in the high peaks as the lightning riddled the skies with white battle fire. White-water rushed down the gulleys, tearing at the moorings of great boulders, uprooting trees. The already saturated earth surrendered to the forces of gravity and collapsed into the gorges, filling the canyon bottoms with mud, debris, rock. Morning dawned feebly through a black, rolling sky.

"Damn." Hamilton Zukor frowned, flipping the curtains to the front window shut.

He had planned on getting the ore shipments out a week ago, now it was doubtful any ore would be moving for a long while. Dent, riding in from the checkpoint had reported that the trail was flooded, impassable for a wagon. He wanted to take the convicts down to clear it. Zukor didn't like the idea, but what else was there to do?

A soft footstep caused Zukor's head to come up. Sylvia stood there in riding cape, tugging her gloves on.

"Where are you going?" Zukor asked.

"Why, down to the ranch," Sylvia replied. "We both agreed it was best, remember?"

The girl seemed nervous for some reason, but that thought did not lodge in Zukor's busy mind. "Yes, yes," he said in response. "But today . . . it's raining like the deluge."

"I'm sure I'll be all right," Sylvia answered briskly. "The roan is a good mudder." Impishly she added, "I know how anxious you were to be rid of me."

"Not at all, not at all," Zukor responded, but it was a relief to see the girl on her way. Sylvia smiled and offered her cheek to her uncle. He kissed it perfunctorily, his thoughts on the ore wagons which were bogged down by this weather.

Sylvia raised her hood, hesitating a moment. The note Shelter Morgan had given her rested in her pocket like a stone. To aid a convict . . . yet what did she owe this man?

Sylvia stepped out into the rain-swept yard, passing a guard on his way in. Zukor watched her go, disappearing through the liquid gray screen.

"They're loaded up and ready," Depew told Zukor.

"What?" Zukor turned distractedly toward the guard.

"Dent told me to load up the prisoners and get that trail cleared off. They're ready to go now."

"All right." The man did not leave immediately and Zukor, irritated, asked, "Is there something else?"

"Morgan . . .? The way the others feel about him?" Depew smiled crookedly and Zukor said, "Oh, I see. All right, take Morgan along. That'll be one less problem to worry about."

Before Depew left, Hamilton Zukor advised him, "My niece is riding out. Make sure she's through the pass, gone before you unload any of those men."

"I will, Mister Zukor." Depew tugged his hat lower, raised the collar of his slicker and stepped off the porch into the driving rain. A rising wind shook the big oaks, drove the raindrops against Depew's face. Turning his head down he sloshed across the yard toward the stable.

Zukor's niece was coming from the stable, riding that pretty roan of hers. Shelter Morgan stood in the doorway, and Depew suppressed a smile. Trying that stuff was he? It would be the last he ever tried.

Shelter's head came around. Silently he watched Depew march toward him through the twisting rain, watched Sylvia disappear into the dark day, the note inside her riding habit.

"You come along with me," Depew said, stepping inside the barn. The rain dripped from his hat and ran along his sharply featured face. Shelter detected a faint smile on Depew's lips, but said nothing.

"Mister Zukor wants the road open. Rain's played hell with his shipping schedule," the guard told Shelter. "We need every man we got."

"All right," Shell said cautiously. He knew the wagons had not gone to the mine that morning, and had known something was up. Still there was an irony in Depew's words he did not like. Shell had found a rain slicker among the smith's abandoned belongings and he shouldered into it. "Do I need any tools?" Morgan asked.

"We'll have plenty down there," Depew said impatiently. "Let's just get moving."

Shelter shrugged and put down the shovel he had picked up. He had turned a quarter away from Depew to lean the shovel against the wall behind the anvil. Depew had seen nothing of the file Shelter Morgan had slipped into the pocket of his slicker.

"Come on," Depew said roughly. "There's a lot to be done on that road today."

In the barracks the men sat sullenly on their beds. Torres had never shaken that cough picked up in the damp mine and from time to time the man's body was racked by it.

"Damned lousy cold," Torres muttered.

"You've got pneumonia, you dumb son of a bitch," Jack Riley snarled.

"You ought to ask Dent to let you off today," Frank Tyler suggested. Torres just smiled back at the kid, shaking his head.

"That would do a lot of damned good."

"I just wish we'd get rolling," Duncan said. The big man was lying flat on his back, making good use of the extra rest time.

The door to the barracks snapped open, driven by the wind. Dent and McGuffie, carrying express guns stood there, rain-slick, chilled.

"Load that wagon," Dent said and McGuffie began moving among them, unlocking the anchor chains. Slowly they hobbled past Dent toward the waiting wagon. Frank Tyler paused.

"Torres shouldn't go out," he told the guard. "It'll kill him."

Dent shrugged and turned his head.

"He's got pneumonia!"

"You'll get worse than that if you don't shut your face and keep moving," Dent told him.

"Thanks, amigo," Torres said.

Frank Tyler turned his disgusted face toward the Mexican, "*Por nada*. Look, take it easy if you can. I'll try to help you."

The rain was fierce. Pitchforks of water stung exposed flesh as they clambered into the uncovered wagon. Bowing their heads they waited until McGuffie had climbed into the box, whipping the team down the trail, Dent and another guard following on horseback.

"Be a nice day to stay inside," Jack Riley spat. His eyes were lifted to the stable. "Be a nice day to tumble in the hay with Zukor's niece and laugh at the poor animals that have to work in the rain."

"Knock it off, Riley," Frank Tyler said.

"Knock it off! I'll knock that son of a bitch's head off if I ever get the chance."

"You don't know . . ." the kid began, but Riley turned on him savagely.

"I know! I got eyes, don't I? Think Zukor takes off these irons because he likes you? Because you been a good boy! The son of a bitch was a government man, Dent told me."

"Like hell," Tyler answered. Duncan glanced at the kid then at Riley who was hopping mad.

"He was, is, you punk!" Riley growled. "Come up here and spent a few weeks workin' with us, then gets tired. So he steps out. Him and Zukor makin' their deal."

"You've got it wrong," Frank Tyler said softly.

"I have! Then tell me, boy, tell me what the hell you know about it."

"I know Morgan—he's no government man, no Zukor man."

"And how do you know that?" Riley badgered him. "How?"

Frank Tyler started to answer, his eyes going to Riley's, to Duncan's then to those of Tex Corson. The rain had washed his hair into his eyes. They were shivering cold; thunder rolled down the hillside.

"I just don't believe it," Frank Tyler said quietly.

Riley sat back, crossing his arms with grim satisfaction. Duncan looked away. The thunder shook the black skies. Banquero sat silently, black eyes fixed to those of Frank Tyler.

They rolled slowly down the mountain, encountering mud slides, debris. Heavy winds rose off the desert, shaking the wagon beneath them. Once the wagon tilted, a wheel sliding over the soft rim of the trail and McGuffie whipped the horses forward, looking back at the thousand foot drop with a sigh of relief.

"They'll have to walk it!" he shouted to Dent. His pointing finger lifted to the trail ahead where a huge boulder had slid off the bank, blocking the trail.

"All right!" Dent hollered above the wind. "This is it. Grab a shovel and step down."

Morosely they stepped to the sodden ground, moving ahead to where the boulder blocked the road. Frank Tyler began digging around the bottom of the huge rock, joined by Corson and Torres. They wanted to loosen the underpinnings of the boulder, slide it off the trail and rebuild the road over the crater that would be left.

In the rain and wind it was a killing proposition. It was most of an hour before the mud had been cleared away and the prisoners, working with levers and muscle slid the boulder off into the deep canyon. Panting, choking, Torres climbed into the wagon, throwing his shovel down.

"What the hell are you doing, Torres?" Dent said savagely. "You boys have just begun. There's a day's work ahead of you."

Helplessly Torres lifted his head, and getting to his knees slid from the wagon bed, his cough shaking his body at intervals.

They walked the rest of the distance to the bottom of the trail. A flash flood had picked up cedar logs, living trees and man-sized rocks, sweeping them down the valley, blocking the trail completely. There was at least a foot of cold, rapidly moving water in the gulley, and two men were knocked off their feet before the job was started, Corson taking a nasty bump on the head as he went down.

Jack Riley unlimbered his shovel and got to work, trying to clear a huge, barkless pine log. He heard the horse splashing toward him and he turned to find Dent there.

"What's the matter?" Riley shouted above the rain.

"I want you up that canyon where the main road bends! Rockslide!"

"All right." Riley looked around. "Just me?"

"There's somebody up there to help you," Dent said evenly. He spun his horse and rode out. Jack Riley breathed a curse, picked up his tools and slopped through the muddy, rapidly-moving water.

Perplexed, Riley glanced over his shoulder, seeing Dent still riding in the opposite direction. No one else was following. Holding his chains high with one hand, Riley forded a small stream and followed the trail around the bend. The wind whistled up the canyons, tearing at the low brush along the bluffs. A rockslide covered half the road, all right, but there was no one else there.

Someone there to help me. Riley scowled and trudged ahead, blinking into the sheeted rain. *Someone* . . . and then he saw him and Jack Riley drew up with a smile.

Shelter Morgan, shovel in his hand, stood watching as Jack Riley approached.

13.

Jack Riley moved steadily forward through the falling rain. Shelter glanced toward him, lifted a hand and hefted a good-sized log, throwing it from the trail as Riley approached, chains clanking.

"I've been waiting for someone to show up", Shelter said. "This stuff is to big to handle alone."

"You won't have to wait no longer," Riley said. As Shell bent over to pick up the other end of the log Riley raised his shovel and arced it through the air, hard.

Shell saw it just in time, rolling aside as the shovel blade, deadly as any guillotine flashed past his shoulder, glancing off the log as the handle splintered in Jack Riley's massive hands.

"Are you crazy!" Shell got quickly to his feet, rubbing the mud from his hands on his slicker. Jack Riley, hunched forward like a bearded grizzly, stood watching him.

"Not much," Riley growled. He had the splintered end of that shovel handle in his hand and he moved forward menacingly. A bear of a man with huge chest and shoulders, Riley was known to have killed four men bare handed. Now, from that look in his dull eyes, he wanted to make it five.

"What is it, Jack?" Shell asked, trying to keep his voice level, confident. Confident was the last thing he felt before Jack Riley. As he spoke Shell's eyes flickered to the ground, beside him, looking for his own shovel, a club of some kind. Riley was moving in, his hair and beard washed with the rain.

"You walked out on us, Morgan. You made fools out of us."

"I don't get you, Jack." Shelter backed slowly away as Riley plodded forward. "They offered me a chance to get those shackles off. Don't tell me you wouldn't have taken it."

"You were in their game all the way, Morgan. Dirty politics, dirty lawmen."

"You got it wrong."

"No." Jack Riley shook his big buffalo's head slowly. "It's not me that's got it wrong, Morgan. It's you."

Shell looked up the rain swept canyon, seeing no

one, no guards, no other prisoners, and it all came clear to him in a flash. Chambers had set him up to be killed. Maybe Zukor had gotten word that there was a marshal planted among the convicts and decided Shelter was the man.

It was clear to Shelter, but it was too late for talking with Jack Riley who had obviously been thinking about this for a long time, and had his mind made up.

The big man lunged and Shelter dropped to the ground, rolling away, only the added awkwardness of Riley's chains slowing his bull-like rush enough to make it possible.

Still Riley caught Shell with a grasping hand, tearing at his shoulder and Shelter knew the time for talking was done. He came to his feet ready. Jack Riley whistled a strong right past Shelter's ear and as Shell stepped inside to evade it, Riley jabbed out with the jagged end of the shovel handle, tearing a gash along Shell's ribs.

Shelter gasped, stepped back and put a hand to his ribs and crouched low, watching the stalking beast through the screen of rain. The footing was muddy and Shell slid as he circled. Riley's thrusting shovel handle flickered out and Shell managed to grab the jagged weapon with his left hand.

But Riley was ox-strong and he jerked it out of Shelter's hand, leaving a deep burn and a deeply embedded splinter in Morgan's palm.

Jack lifted the handle again and smashed it down against Shelter's shoulder at the base of the neck, moving in at the same time to strike out with a meaty left. Big as Riley was, he was a split second slower then Shell who was able to duck inside the left.

Shoulder aching, Shell stepped back, fending Riley off with open hands. Yet he could sense that this was no way to go about it. Riley was fighting mad, primed to kill, and Shell would have to fight as if his life was on the line.

He stopped suddenly, and kicked out hard with a bootheel catching Riley on the kneecap, but the man must have been made of iron, the bone did not break and Riley only flinched, coming in steadily.

Shell backed away, peppering Riley's chin with jabs, then doubling with a pair of uppercuts which only grazed the big man's chin. Shell felt the bluff behind him, and he knew he could back no farther. Jack still had that murderously splintered shovel handle, and the first objective had to be to get it away from him; a man could be skewered on its deadly point.

Shell went into a crouch, the muddy bluff behind him, Riley feinting then moving ominously forward. Riley jabbed out with the shovel handle and Shell rolled to one side. Again he tried it, with all the bulk of his upper body behind it, but this time Shell was able to find the opening he wanted. As Riley struck, Shell slapped down, gripping Riley's forearm with his left, his hand with his right. Then shoving back hard on Riley's hand he was able to break the grip, the shovel handle falling free as Riley's wrist cracked.

But Riley was far from finished. Damaged wrist or not, he was determined, angry, capable. He threw an elbow which caught Shelter on the nose, breaking it. Shell's face was showered with blood, and Riley followed by mauling Shell with a series of overhand rights. There was force behind those blows and he staggered Shelter who backed away, covering up.

Yet Riley was too confident, perhaps too angry. He marched in, slamming rights and lefts at Shell who caught most of them on his arms and shoulders, still giving ground as the two men fought through the mud and rain.

Riley was a savage bear just then, the rain streaming down his face as he levelled a barrage of vicious rights and lefts at Shelter who backed away, taking his time. Now and then Shell stabbed a left into Jack Riley's nose, keeping the big man back a step, but for the most part he was content to let Riley throw his best shots, tiring himself.

Riley winged a right and Shell answered with a crisp left hook which flattened Riley's ear. A second hook glanced off the big man's temple and a third caught him flush on the jaw.

Riley blinked and moved in again. Slightly staggered by Shelter's last shot, he tried not to indicate it, yet Shell could read it in his eyes. Having him wobbly, Shell wanted him. Now, before he could gain a full head of steam again.

Shelter blocked a straight right with his forearm and stepped in, ducking his head. It could be deadly to trade punches with the big man, but Shelter wanted him now. He went downstairs, to Riley's wind, finding him firmer than he had guessed. Still Riley didn't like it and he lowered his guard.

Shell stepped back, jabbed out and then rolled a head-splitting right over Riley's guard and the big man went down.

Riley went flat on his pants into the deep mud, but he was not built to quit and he jumped up again, staggering as he came at Shelter.

Riley threw a wild right, hoping for the kill, but Shelter was too quick for him and his own right, triggered a split second before Riley's, sent the big man to the mud again.

This time it was face down and Riley rose slowly, his bearded face and chest a mass of mud. "It's over, Jack. Let's talk it out now," Shelter said. His own fists were split, his head ringing.

"There's nothin' to talk over," Riley panted. His massive chest rose and fell heavily. "If only I'd a had a gun, Morgan . . ."

He drove forward again, and Shell caught him on the point of the chin. It was a stiff left, with all of Shelter's shoulder weight behind it and Riley stopped dead, like a steer meeting a sledge hammer. His eyes rolled back and Shell watched him warily as Riley's knees came undone and he toppled forward, again landing in the foot deep mud, the rain washing over him.

Jack Riley was many things, but never a quitter. He got to his knees, tried to rise, but he could not make it. He flopped down again, rolling onto his back, buried in the red mud.

Panting, Shelter stood over him. Then, reaching down he jerked Riley up by the collar and dragged him out of the center of the road to where the mud was not so deep. He propped Jack up against a boulder and sat down himself, his arms shaky.

Riley's eyes came open heavily. Shelter asked him, "Now can we talk?"

"There's nothin' to say. You crossed us. And nothin' can convince me otherwise."

Shelter shook his head, lifted one of Jack's heavy feet and got to work. "What the hell are you doin'?" Riley wanted to know.

"Tryin' to convince you, Jack," Shelter answered.

Riley could see now what Morgan was doing. With a file he had produced from somewhere the blond man was taking long even strokes over the head of the retaining pin on Riley's leg irons.

"What for?" Riley asked through split, puffy lips. "Why are you doing that?"

"So you can get the hell out of here, you big donkey," Shell said without looking up from his work. The head of the first pin was nearly through and with a rock and the file Shelter was able to knock the shackle off.

"You're no lawman," Riley said slowly.

"You're right."

Shelter shifted to the other leg, filing at the pin as the rain fell in constant sheets. Shell's eyes went to the north end of the pass as he worked, expecting to see Dent and his men appear at any time. He worked hurriedly, leaning back with relief as the second pin fell free, the rusted leg iron dropping from Jack Riley's swollen, raw ankle.

"I don't get you, Morgan," the big man said finally.

Shelter stared at Riley through the rain, his hair in his eyes. "They were using you, Jack," he explained. "You against me. Wanting to get rid of both of us, I guess. They had the crazy idea I was a marshal."

"And I believed 'em," Jack said apologetically.

"It happens."

"Shell . . ."

"Best get up and get movin', Jack. They'll be comin' soon to see if you've done your chore."

"Yeah." Riley stood, testing his legs, still watching Shelter with bafflement. "What about you?"

"I'm going back up the mountain," Shell said, and Riley burst into a short, disbelieving laugh which broke off abruptly as he realized that Shelter was serious.

"You mean it. But why?" Riley spread his hands.

"That promise I made Banquero."

"Banquero!" Riley boomed a derisive laugh. "That you'd get him out of here?"

"That's right," Shell acknowledged.

"I guess I wasn't readin' you right before," Riley said. The two men faced each other through the steady rain. "I thought you were halfway smart. Hell, you're plain crazy, Morgan. That Apache, he's as liable to turn on you and cut your throat as he is thank you. Assuming you could bust him free somehow—which I'm thinkin' is likely as hair on a bullfrog."

"I expect you're right," Shelter had to admit. "But I spoke up, I made the man a promise."

"Yeah." Riley nodded slowly. "Well, that's where you made your mistake, Morgan. Good luck." Jack Riley turned and tromped off through the mud, heading due south. Then he stopped, glanced back and slowly turned. He walked slowly back toward Shelter, muttering, "Mexico's too damned far to walk. I'm going to see if I can snag a pony."

"Up on the mountain?" Shell asked with a grin.

"Don't see none runnin' loose down here," Riley growled. "I'm kickin' myself, you know."

"Yeah."

Cautiously they worked their way back toward the fork in the road, walking along the bluffs. The storm clouds parted once, splashing a brilliant sunspot against the mountain briefly before the rolling black skies swallowed it up again.

Shelter froze, getting down on his belly. Jack Riley crouched and moved up beside him. It was cold, uncomfortable, but Shelter had seen the shadowy figure moving up the road and had no wish to be seen himself.

It was Depew, riding slowly through the mist, his slicker black, trailing back over the haunches of the Appaloosa he rode. Under that slicker he had a Winchester.

"He's comin' to check," Shell said and Riley nodded.

"Want to go for him?"

"If he gets off a shot, we're done," Shell said soberly.

"He won't get off a shot."

They slipped back from the bluff, racing through the muddy, brush heavy ravines, Riley's panting loud in Shelter's ears. There was a chance. If they took him at the bend, and took him quickly.

The thunder roared again and the brush trembled before it, the rain slanting steadily down. It was dark in the canyons, cold and blustery. Depew was in no mood for any of this. He would as soon plug Morgan and Riley both, forgetting this fancy business.

His mind was on the hot coffee he never got that morning, on the girl named Rhonda who worked at the Trail's End. The Appy beneath him slipped in the mud and plodded on.

Depew made the sharp bend in the trail and pulled up with a yank on the reins. Lying face down in the mud was Shelter Morgan. Depew smiled grimly and eased the pony forward. He never saw the huge, moving shadow leap from the brush at the side of the trail, he was so intent on Morgan.

Riley hit him high, knocking the guard from his horse which bucked away, kicking up its heels at Jack Riley and Depew hit the muddy ground in a rolling, tumbling splash. The wind went out of Depew as Riley landing on top of him, but he was alert enough to grab for his Colt.

Depew was to his feet, the hammer on that Colt back as Riley stood, trying to shake off the effects of the fall. "So long," Depew said.

It was then that he heard the sound of a rapid footstep, and in panic he realized who it was. *Set up*.

It was the last thought of Depew's brief life. Shelter Morgan hit the guard hard from the back, his right hand arcing over, plunging against Depew's chest and the guard went down, eyes open to the falling rain, the file driven deep into his blood soaked chest.

167

Riley got slowly to his feet, and came forward, studying Depew. Glancing at Shelter he said softly, "That's a damned useful tool."

Shelter bent over and took the Colt revolver from Depew's curled hand. It was cocked and he showed it to Jack Riley.

"Close," the big man breathed.

Shelter dropped the hammer easily and tucked the pistol into his belt. Then he retrieved Depew's muddy Winchester and tossed it to Jack Riley. "There's your horse, Jack," Shelter told him. The Appaloosa stood, head down not twenty feet away, surveying the two men with anxious brown eyes.

"Yeah." Riley started to say something, but didn't. He lifted a hand and walked to the ground-tethered horse, taking up the reins.

Shelter had grabbed hold of Depew's body and he dragged him off the road, concealing him behind a tangle of brush. When Shelter looked up Riley was still there.

"What's up, Jack?" He lifted a finger. "Border's that way."

"I don't speak no Mexican anyway," Riley shrugged. He looked to the mountains, shrouded in silver cloud at this late hour. "You think we can do it?"

"Hell, I don't know. Haven't tried it yet," Shell grinned.

"Well. I guess if we're going to try, we'd best have at it." Riley peered at the skies. "It'll be comin' dark real fast now."

Shelter nodded, grinning again. Riley watched as Morgan bent over again and stripped the slicker from Depew's body. "See his hat anywhere, Jack?"

Riley pointed with the rifle to a hollow across the road where Depew's battered, soaked hat lay. He picked it up, brushed off the loose mud and planted it on his head, shouldering into Depew's slicker.

"Well?" Shelter asked.

"Don't look much like him," Riley said pensively.

"Like you say—it's comin' dark."

They switched guns, Riley tucking the Colt behind his belt in back, Shell taking the Winchester as he stepped into the Appaloosa's saddle, hoping he would look enough like Depew in this light to get them within range.

"More walkin'," Jack Riley grumbled as they headed out. "You could have let me be Depew, bringin' you back."

"Uh-uh. I'm supposed to be dead, remember? You did a good job on me."

"If you'd a killed me," Riley complained, "at least I could've rode."

"Could be it won't make any difference," Shelter told him. The horse splashed on through the mud and water. "Could be Dent will see to it we're both dead for real. Then it won't make no great shakes about the horse."

Jack nodded his head in silent agreement. They were at the fork in the road once more. Once across the white-water ford and around the bend there was no turning back. Riley stopped, looked up the trail and then took a deep breath, fording the creek. He took the time to mutter, "I never knew you could *catch* loco."

169

14.

Dusk was coloring the high clouds. The rain had finally halted, at least for the time being. Dent pulled his watch from his pocket, grumbled a curse and tucked it away.

The convicts were finishing with the road. The crater left by the boulder had been filled in, packed and was now being levelled. McGuffie stifled a yawn as Dent's eyes met his. The third guard, Liggett sat on the tail gate of the wagon, watching the prisoners with brooding eyes.

The wind was cold in the canyon and Dent turned his collar up.

He glanced down the road again impatiently, expecting Depew. Old D.D. was a good man, Dent decided, but he could screw up an anvil at times.

Dent started to give the signal to load the convicts,

and then he saw them. Depew was riding behind Jack Riley, bringing black beard home. Dent smiled. It had worked, then. They were all in the clear — the convict had killed another prisoner. How could they have known he was a marshal? Not that it was likely any information had gotten out. Still, better to play it safe.

Dent lifted a hand and Depew lifted an answering hand. "Load 'em up, McGuffie," Dent ordered.

He took a step down the trail, watching as Depew drew nearer, rifle across the withers of that Appaloosa. Jack Riley looked some beat up — Morgan must have put up a fight.

A glance told Dent that McGuffie had the prisoners loading onto the wagon. He turned again to watch Jack Riley, walking with that waddle-gait a man in chains uses . . . but he wasn't in chains!

Dent's eyes popped wide open and he looked at Depew, feeling a cold chill run the length of his spine. Dent dropped his hickory club and grabbed for his sidearm.

"McGuffie! Liggett!" he had time to shout out before Shelter Morgan's rifle went to his shoulder, Jack Riley taking three quick steps to the side, whipping his Colt from behind his belt.

Dent got his handgun into action quickly, but it was not quick enough. He felt the fire of Shelter's shot explode in his upper chest just as he pulled the trigger himself.

Dent's shot went wild, whining off the rocks above. His shirt front was soaked in blood, the acrid smell of gunpowder filled his nostrils.

Behind him he head a burst of gunfire, but he did not turn to see what had happened. Clutching his shoulder Dent took a rubbery step forward, lifting his Colt once more. The hammer was heavy, cold beneath his thumb as he pulled it back.

He brought it level and touched off again, seeing Morgan who had not taken the Winchester from his shoulder disappear behind a puff of black powder smoke from the rifle.

Then it was very cold. Dent stuck out a hand and was surprised to find it filled with mud. He didn't remember falling, being hit again, but now the searing pain in his chest burst through his body.

Dent looked up, saw Morgan outlined against the sky, watched as Morgan and the horse whirled around, going black. His hand twitched once more and then Dent was dead—the red, cold mud painting his face.

At the first shot from Dent, Jack Riley had gone to a knee, seeing Shelter's quick reaction from the corner of his eye.

McGuffie, surprised and confused, had gone for the express gun in the wagon box, but Jack had punched three shots through the man with that Colt .44.

Someone else had fired. Riley glanced around, assuring himself Morgan was still alive, then he made a rush for the wagon.

Leaping into the bed, Jack Riley came to an abrupt stop. Liggett was there on the floor of the wagon. Sitting above him was Duncan and the giant had his leg irons stretched across the guard's throat.

Liggett wriggled furiously, clutching at his throat, his eyes wide, pleading. But Duncan had no mercy—not just then—and he pressed down still harder, the black iron strangling the life from Liggett.

Frank Tyler leaped to the wagon bed, took one quick look then murmured, "For God's sake, Duncan!"

Duncan shoved the kid aside as if brushing away a fly. Liggett was utterly white, his throat bruised, torn. His hands were still on the chain, yet those hands no longer fought.

"Is he dead?" Duncan asked Jack Riley.

"If he ain't, he ain't gonna *get* dead," Jack said in an awed voice.

"That's what I thought." Duncan rose, lifting the chain from Liggett's horribly mangled throat. Then with incredible ease the big man picked Liggett's corpse up and threw it. It went bouncing down the muddy canyons, a pair of muffled thumps rising as it settled.

Banquero sat silently eyeing them all as Shelter Morgan rode to the wagon. Slowly Shelter swung down, tossing his rifle to Frank Tyler.

Deliberately Shelter walked to where Banquero sat and he lifted the Chiricahua's leg, holding it like a smith holds a pony's hoof. Taking the file from his slicker Shell worked steadily on the pins until both ankles were free.

Shell picked up the irons, holding them for Banquero to study. "Here is my promise," Shelter said.

Banquero's face was unreadable. A cool amusement seemed to flash in those coal black eyes. "Tell him!" Shelter said across his shoulder to Jim Fox.

"He knows. Banquero knows what you've said," Fox replied.

"Good." Shell nodded and turned to Fox with the file. "Why don't you do Frank and then let him do you."

"First . . ." a weak voice gasped. It was Torres, his face drawn, eyes glassy and they turned to look at him. "Do me first, Morgan. I don't want to die with these on."

That deep, frame-racking cough of the Mexican's flared up then, and they stood looking at Torres. He was not long for it, they all could see it.

"All right," Shelter said. "Torres first, Fox."

Jim Fox nodded and went to where Torres sat sagged against the cold earth. The breed filed the pins as the others watched.

"Damn waste of time," Jack Riley grumbled. Then he turned away so that no one could see the moisture in his eyes.

The skies were only partly cloudy. A dull, rising moon glittered on the desert floor as the last flush of scarlet sundown painted the high crowns of the dying stormclouds.

Duncan was the last man to have his shackles dropped and when they hit the earth it was full dark, only the hazy moon illuminating the night, their haggard faces.

"And what now?" Duncan asked. He had Liggett's handgun thrust into his belt.

"Zukor," Tex Corson said angrily. "I'll have his head."

"That's a futile feather for your warbonnet," Frank Tyler said from the darkness. "Go back up that mountain? Kill Zukor. Run. You're gaining nothing, losing only time. You can make a run of it now, Tex. The border's not far."

"I can't see him get away with it," Corson said. He looked toward Torres who had ceased his tortured breathing. "The Mex and me were friends."

"He won't get away with it," Frank Tyler vowed.

"That's easy enough to say," Jack Riley grumbled.

"He won't!" Tyler repeated, and they looked at the kid with disbelief.

Shelter Morgan stepped forward, holding that Winchester. He looked to Duncan and then to Tyler. "I'm adding my word to Frank's," Shelter said. "Zukor won't get away with this. There'll never be another man wearing irons here. You're blowing your own chances by going back up."

It was Jack Riley who stood then, facing Duncan and the others. "You can rest easy about it, Dunc," Jack said. "If Morgan gives his word, Zukor's as good as done. I seen what his word means."

"All right." Duncan stood heavily, his legs still swollen, sore. "Let's get it rolling then. Tex?"

Corson nodded. "Sure."

They piled into the wagon, with Shelter on the Appaloosa leading the way. Jack Riley had caught up Liggett's horse. Frank Tyler had Dent's bay gelding.

They splashed across the creek, Tyler riding close to Shelter Morgan. "You know what you're doing?" Shell asked the kid through the darkness. "Helping convicted killers, bandits get away?"

"No," Frank Tyler whispered tautly. "I don't know what the hell I'm doing! Only that these men, rough as they are, have become my friends." They rode silently for a time, through the dark canyon, the pale moon pasted to a gray sky.

"Thanks, Morgan," Frank Tyler said eventually.

"For what?"

"For everything. *You* sprung us. You took my risks. You kept quiet about who I was . . . thanks."

"All right. You owe me one," Shelter answered.

"What do you want?"

"I'm holding it in reserve," Shell grinned. "Okay?"

"Okay." Tyler nodded, slowing his horse slightly as Shelter did. The checkpoint was just ahead, far beyond that, the lights of Strawberry, brilliant against the darkness. It was incredible to think that men lived in that town. Free men with their feet on a bar rail, with wives at home, a gun on their belt, no need to look over their shoulders at the sound of approaching foot steps.

"Ahead," Shelter nodded. Jack Riley had come up beside them and the bearded man peered into the darkness. "If there's anyone around, it will be here."

Slowly then they rolled on toward the checkpoint, every man alert, Shelter's hand firm on the Winchester. But Yawkey was not at the gate. It was chained, locked, but there were no guards.

"Bust it down!" Duncan yelled. He leaped from the wagon. "That's the freedom road stretched out tuther side."

They had to use the three saddle horses and all of their weight, but finally the heavy gate was uprooted and thrown aside. The wagon pulled ahead and Duncan, Tex and Banquero climbed back aboard.

"Now," Jack Riley said, "let's put some distance between us and this place."

They rode through the moonlit night, descending toward the desert floor, with Strawberry, well-lighted now, on their left, the moon to their right.

"There's a road south, ain't there?" Riley asked as he rode beside Shell, the wagon behind them.

"There is." Shell lifted a hand to the low hills.

"Run to the border, does it?"

"It runs to Fort Bowie. It's not far from there to Mexico."

It was another hour to the Fort Bowie cut-off where it all had begun for Shelter. He looked down the sliver of moon-glossed road, recalling how it had been with Penny and old Ben Dolittle.

Shelter swung down, leading the horse back under the oaks which were on a low rise. The dust they had stirred up was settling now, and there was no other dust visible for miles. They had made it, made it clean.

The others got down from the wagon, walking toward Shelter. Corson lifted a finger. "See them dark mountains? That's Mexico. There's a town called Zapata about fifty miles down. Once laid up there with a woman. She made some enchiladas . . . if she's still there, I'm tryin' it again. I won't be back across the line, not on a bet."

"What about you, Duncan?" Jim Fox asked.

"I never been to Mexico, but it's got to look better than a gallows. I'm ridin' with Tex if he don't mind."

"Shelter?"

Shell glanced up. He was crouched down, scratching at the earth with a twig. "Not me, boys. I've got some battles up here."

"You're crazy then," Jack Riley told him., "Go into Strawberry and they'll hang you—as legal as they'd hang me."

"I know it." Shelter stood. "Still, I owe some folks."

"Them promises you keep making are going to get you killed some day," Riley told him seriously. "Ride south with us."

"No. Can't do it. You boys ride light, watch the backtrail."

"Frank?" Tex Corson asked. The kid shook his head.

"I'm riding with Morgan back to Strawberry," the kid replied.

"You're loco!" Riley said. "Shelter got you makin' those promises too?"

"Sort of." Frank Tyler looked the bearded man in the eye. "It's my job, you see. I'm the law, Jack."

Riley laughed, but Duncan did not. Tex Corson took a step backward as if someone had shoved him.

"You!" Riley scoffed.

"That's right, Jack. I'm the Federal man they were lookin' for."

"You knew?" Riley asked Shelter Morgan.

"I knew," Shell nodded.

"Why didn't you just tell us . . . ?" Riley was baffled again. Morgan was either shorter on smarts or longer on guts than any man he had met. Putting the finger on the kid would have saved the blond man a lot of grief.

"I don't like it," Duncan said. He was scowling deeply, his silver hair in his eyes. "Leavin' a lawman behind to say where we were going."

"As far as I'm concerned," Frank Tyler told Duncan, "you boys have done your time in Hell. Whatever you've done, you've paid for it."

"Smooth talkin'," Duncan replied sharply. "Who's to say you won't pick up some fresh men and horses and be on our trail come dawn? That wagon won't be movin' that fast."

"The kid says it," Morgan interrupted, standing to face Duncan. "*I* say it. Won't nobody be comin' after you, Dunc."

"That another promise?" Jack Riley asked with just the faintest smile. Shelter looked at the outlaw through the darkness and slowly nodded.

"It is, Jack."

"That ain't good enough," Duncan snapped.

"It is for me," Jack said. "If Morgan gives his word, it's iron-clad. Ask Banquero . . ."

Riley looked around and frowned. Banquero was gone. No one had seen the Apache slip away, yet he probably had felt no interest in this white man's council. He was free and he intended to stay free.

"Be damned," Jim Fox muttered. Then the breed said to Duncan. "Let's get rolling, Dunc. We're wastin' time."

"That the way you feel about it, Tex?" Duncan asked Corson.

"It is," Tex told him. "I trust Morgan, and it's time to be movin'."

Without another word Duncan turned and stamped off toward the wagon. Tex tipped his hat and followed. "Ride loose, Shelter," Jim Fox said, and then he too was gone, and Shelter watched as they whipped the team, the wagon rolling southward on the Fort Bowie cut-off.

"Thanks, Jack," Shelter said.

"It was nothin'," Jack Riley shrugged. "Old Dunc, he's full of hot air."

"Yeah," Frank Tyler said thoughtfully, "I've seen some of his hot air."

"But you two are really going after Chambers?"

Jack Riley asked. "Just the two of you?"

"That's right," Shelter said. He walked to the Appaloosa, tightening the cinch again as Jack watched.

"I'd *like* to help . . ." Riley apologized.

"I understand," Shelter said, swinging into the saddle.

"It's my hide I'm talkin' about," Jack Riley said. "I don't want to hang, or go through nothin' like that back there again."

"Can't blame you," Shelter said. The moonlight was on his lean face. The desert was still. "Ready, Frank."

"Uh-huh." Tyler was in the saddle beside Shelter. Jack Riley looked up to them.

"You understand, don't you, Frank?" the bearded man asked.

"Of course I do," the kid answered.

"Couldn't be no other way."

"No." Shelter Morgan lifted a hand. "Luck to you, Jack."

Shelter turned his pony toward Strawberry, Frank Tyler beside him. They had ridden a hundred yards before they heard the driving hoofbeats behind them and Shelter pulled up. Jack Riley fell in silently beside them and they rode on, heading for the twinkling, distant lights of Strawberry.

15.

Luke was tilted back in a chair in the living room of the old house. The fire was burning low and it was late. He fought off a yawn, ran a hand back across his balding head and shifted slightly in the chair.

He had closed his eyes again, letting his thoughts wander back to Dallas and a girl in a gold dress when he heard the latch on the front door and he came to his feet, gun in hand.

"Who is it?" Luke asked, standing to one side of the door.

"Me. Open up," a voice answered, and recognizing it, the deputy swung open the door to the Dawkins' house to admit Wes Chambers.

The sheriff came through the door quickly, his eyes taking in the room, its old furnishings, his deputy.

"Everything quiet?" Chambers asked.

"Quiet as death so far," Luke shrugged. He

holstered his gun and locked the door behind Chambers. "Ain't heard a peep out of them." He nodded toward the closed bedroom door.

"They're still there, aren't they?" Chambers asked, a flash of uneasiness running across him.

"No way to get out, Sheriff. Besides, from time to time I take a peek through the keyhole."

"Good." Chambers paced the carpet, tipping his hat back. He was worried, uncomfortable with the decision he had to make. If he was found out in this . . .

"It's a bear, ain't it?" Luke asked. Chambers glanced at the bald man but did not answer.

"I guess there ain't an easy way out of this," Chambers said, as much to himself as to Luke.

"What about the Zukor girl?" Luke asked. He had taken up his perch in the chair once more.

"She's still here!"

"I wasn't going to make no decision on that, Wes."

"No." Wes Chambers eyed his deputy. He shrugged, "There's nothing to be done about her. It'll have to be up to Zukor to do what he wants. You sure she never read that note from Morgan?"

"That's what she says," Luke answered doubtfully.

Chambers turned toward the fireplace, eyes narrowing. They had been keeping an eye on Penny Dolittle, with the thought that she might have been connected with Shelter Morgan, with the U.S. marshals. They had about abandoned that notion, figuring the girl was telling the truth about going into those red hills just to get a few things when Zukor's niece showed up . . . with a note from Morgan.

Chambers rolled a smoke in agitation. The note had been burned, but he recalled it word for word.

* * *

"Penny, get in touch with Federal authorities. Slave camp at Canyon Rim, and me one. Tell them their man Tyler still alive, up here too."

Shell

"I'd best talk to them again. Get that Sylvia Woods out here, would ya, Luke."

Luke got slowly to his feet and crossed the room, opening the bedroom door. The three women's heads came up sharply. Old Mrs. Dawkins had a hard look on her lined face. Luke was glad she didn't have a gun in her hand.

"Sheriff wants you, Miss Woods."

Sylvia stood slowly. Her dark eyes went to Penny and to Mrs. Dawkins. She patted her raven hair and walked slowly to the door, Luke's eyes on her, sweeping down that voluptuous figure.

"You'll never get away with this Luke Weese," Mrs. Dawkins said, her voice hard-edged.

"With what, Ma'm?" the deputy smiled. "We're only conducting an investigation."

"I'm a prisoner in my own house!" Mrs. Dawkins said stiffly.

"Sheriff thought it was more seemly than taking you down to the jail, Ma'm." Luke smiled again, a jackal's smile. "Ought to be more careful with the boarders you take in." He glanced at Penny Dolittle who stood hands on hips, glaring back; laughing, he locked the door.

Wes Chambers looked around slowly. She was a beautiful woman, Zukor's niece. Her breasts rose and fell with the emotions inside of her, the firelight sparked in her eyes.

"What is it?" she demanded. "Are you going to set me free, Sheriff?"

"Of course," Chambers said with mock surprise. "Why, we've nothing in the world against you, Miss Woods. We're just tryin' to get to the bottom of things."

Sylvia returned the man's stare icily. He motioned for her to be seated, but she remained standing before the fire.

"All right," Chambers said, "we'll get on with it. What it comes down to is that you were smuggling a note from a prisoner into town."

"I didn't look at it as smuggling," Sylvia said haughtily. Her eyebrows were arched over cool eyes. "Nor did I know the man was a prisoner. The stablehand asked me to deliver a note to his sweetheart," she lied.

"Penny Dolittle?"

"Yes," Sylvia nodded.

"Did you read the note?" Chambers asked, trying to make his voice casual.

"I am not in the habit of reading other people's love letters," Sylvia answered. Chambers locked eyes with the woman, trying to find that hint of a lie in her expression. She stared back indignantly.

"Then this man trusted you . . . this stablehand?" Chambers persisted.

"I couldn't say whether he did or not. Probably I was simply the first person by who was not a guard. Frankly, Sheriff, this is all a little tedious. I'm sure my Uncle Hamilton will not like this a bit. Not one bit!"

"You can bet you're right there," Chambers muttered. He unfolded a paper from his vest pocket and handed it to Sylvia who glanced at the wanted poster.

"Shelter Morgan?"

"Yes. Is that the man who gave you the note?"

Sylvia sighed and scanned the poster. "Yes, yes, although I couldn't testify as to the scar on his thigh." There was a mockery in her words and Chambers frowned, wondering.

"So you see, Miss Woods, that stablehand was a very dangerous man. A murderer trying to contact his girlfriend. You were implicated. I had to hold you for questioning."

"And now the questioning is at an end?"

"Yes."

"Then I am free to go," Sylvia said, turning sharply.

"Yes . . . and no," Chambers answered. "I've sent a man to your uncle. Mister Zukor will have to take custody of you, you see."

"No," she flared up, "I don't see."

"Well," Chambers shrugged, "that's the way it is. It's a dangerous land out there— plenty of hard men. One might try to take advantage of you," he said, his eyes greedily running over her.

Sylvia replied with utter coldness, "He'd have to be a hell of a man." Her eyes were disparaging, piercing.

Chambers waved a disgusted hand. "Lock her up, Luke." The deputy rose and Sylvia objected vehemently.

"I thought I was no longer a prisoner!"

"You aren't," Chambers said with a pretense of dismay. "As I've said, we're simply holding you —for your own protection—until your uncle can see you safely home."

"You can't!" Sylvia protested, but she knew full well that Wes Chambers could. He could do as he liked in all the territory between Steamboat and Bowie. There was no other law but his.

"Luke." Wes Chambers nodded and the deputy took Sylvia by the arm, leading her back to the bedroom. Penny's eyes snapped up as Luke came in. He watched as Sylvia sat down, but he did not leave.

"Are you quite through?" Mrs. Dawkins asked harshly. A peppery woman who had come across the Plains in '54 with her husband, and had seen Comanche attacks, gunfights, border wars, she had no give in her and no use for men like Luke or Wes Chambers.

"If you and the girl will come with me, Ma'am," Luke answered.

"Penny and I?"

"That's right. The girl is a suspect in an escape plot."

"And I suppose I am guilty by being her employer and landlady?" Mrs. Dawkins erupted.

"No one says you are guilty of anything, Mizz Dawkins. It's just the sheriff wants you to come along down to the jailhouse . . . to sign a deposition."

"A deposition!" the old woman snorted. "Wes Chambers never had use for such fancy frills before, and as for you, Luke Weese, I doubt you have an idea what the word means."

The deputy flushed deeply and Penny noticed it. Luke Weese wasn't much, but he had been known to use violence when and where it pleased him. Penny took Mrs. Dawkins' arm.

"We'd best go along with the sheriff, Mrs.

Dawkins," Penny Dolittle said.

"All right. All right! Let me get my shawl," she said testily. Wrapping it around her shoulders, the old woman followed Penny and Luke into the parlor where Chambers waited.

Earl Weese had arrived in the meantime along with Farrell, Chambers' head deputy, and Penny looked them over angrily.

"You need all these men just to take two ladies to the jailhouse?"

"It's not because of you, Miss Dolittle," Chambers said. "The boys just happened by. We've been having a little meeting."

"Sure," Penny responded, and suddenly, looking over the deputies, she had a cold foreboding. Her heart skipped twice and she glanced at Mrs. Dawkins who was calm, her shawl clutched around her shoulders.

"I don't like this," Farrell said aside to Chambers.

"You like ending up on a chain gang yourself?" Wes hissed back. "The girl's wise to us."

Farrell lifted his eyes to the little mouse of a girl in the oversized coat and undergrowed figure. Penny's eyes met his and he turned them down again rapidly.

"It's full dark," Chambers said, "let's get moving."

Luke shut the door to the room where Sylvia was being held, leaning his back against it. Chambers and Earl Weese whipped out torn strips of rag, and they gagged and blindfolded Penny and Mrs. Dawkins.

"Quietly now," Wes Chambers cautioned them

and Earl opened the front door, glancing up and down Main Street which was quiet.

"It's clear, Wes," he said.

"All right. You stay with Zukor's niece. Don't let anyone in."

Chambers nodded to Farrell who blew out the lantern before they made their move. Penny, held tightly by Wes Chambers, was shoved through the front door and down onto the street. She missed her step and was yanked to her feet again.

Chambers turned his men into the first alley behind the hardware store, and they angled across the littered vacant lot toward the railroad tracks beyond.

Joe Farrell searched the darkness uneasily. He liked none of this, but he didn't have what it took to challenge Wes Chambers over it.

It was cold, their breath steamed from their lips. The ground underfoot was sodden with the heavy rains, the skies clear. A steer lowed in the cattle pens beyond the depot.

They were nearly there. Farrell knew where they were going although he hadn't asked and hadn't been told. It was a place Wes Chambers had used before. Lewis Hart was there.

The cistern had been dug by the railroad years earlier, and it sat beside the falling-down shack which had been the original depot. The well was dry now, abandoned, deep.

A long, sheer cloud was flagged across the rising half moon. Farrell flinched, thinking he had seen a movement, a running shadow, but when he looked again there was nothing.

Nerves, he told himself. Right then Joe Farrell made himself a vow—this was the last night he'd work for Wes Chambers. Come morning he was riding, far and fast.

The old woman stumbled and Luke jerked her upright. A bank of tumbleweeds rested against the old wire fence. Beyond the fence the depot was silent.

"Joe!" Wes Chambers hissed impatiently.

Farrell had the key to the lock on the cistern cover, and the sheriff waited restlessly while Joe fumbled for it and worked at the rusty lock.

Penny and Mrs. Dawkins stood silently, blindfolded with Chambers and Luke Weese holding them tightly. Luke had slipped his bowie knife from its sheath. Glancing around nervously, he watched as Farrell freed the lock and lifted the heavy cistern cover.

"Where are we?" Penny asked, suddenly terrified.

"At the gate to Hell," Wes Chambers said sadistically.

But his words never had the effect he had planned. On their heels came an answering, quiet voice from the shadows.

"Then you'd better jump on in, Chambers. Jump in or I'll blast you right through that gate."

16.

Chambers froze, his eyes opening wide. He could not see the man who had spoken, but he knew the voice well enough.

Morgan.

Chambers had frozen, but Luke Weese had not. He was filled with utter panic, caught in the most heinous crime a frontier man could commit —murdering women. Luke saw nothing more than Chambers could, but he was not waiting. His Colt came up and he banged off two shots at the shadows, aiming for where he thought the voice had come from.

The shots brought instant reactions from Chambers and Joe Farrell who had been frozen into immobility. Farrell had drawn his pistol as well, but he had no intention of making a fight of it. He had only one thing on his mind. He started running.

It was a fatal error. A single shot boomed out from behind the old depot and Farrell felt the violent impact of hot lead. He clutched his chest, clawed at the air and tumbled forward, his head slamming against the rim of the cistern.

He was already dead as his body plummeted down the dark, moss slick shaft to the pond of stagnant water far below.

"That's enough!" Shell yelled. "Give it up, Chambers."

"Like hell!"

Chambers shot three times, as rapidly as he could fan the hammer of his Colt, shattering the night with roaring gunfire, splintering the wall of the depot before taking off at a dead run toward the railroad tracks beyond.

Shelter sent a following shot after Chambers, but by now the women were in line and he had to lower his gun.

Luke had made his own move simultaneously. He had his bowie out and Penny as a hostage, but he had no idea he could bluff it out. He started backing away, dropping the knife as he filled his hand with his Smith & Wesson.

A huge shadowy figure charged out of the darkness and Luke whirled, shoving Penny hard, into the path of the onrushing Jack Riley.

Penny, bound and gagged, slammed into Riley who caught her with his massive bear arms. Luke ducked, let go with a pair of searching shots toward the depot and took to his heels, Shelter in hot pursuit.

Wes Chambers had already faded into the shadows around the new depot and the stockyards beyond. Luke was far ahead of Shelter and the deputy wheeled once, throwing a wild shot in Shell's direction.

Shelter stopped dead, slowly raised his Colt and thumbed back the hammer. He took a small breath and squeezed off a shot at the fleeing gunman.

The shot echoed through the night, followed by an agonized scream from Luke Weese. It was a leg shot, and he hobbled on, climbing the depot platform as Shelter fired again, this shot smashing the glass from the window of the empty depot, ricocheting angrily off something metallic within.

Shelter made the platform, and leaning against the wall of the depot he ejected his three spent cartridges, shoveling fresh ammunition into the cylinder of the blue Colt.

A faint breeze stirred the big oaks beyond the tracks where a string of boxcars lay dead on the track. The moon was screened by high clouds, the only sounds were the beating of Shelter's heart and the far off calling of an owl.

Shelter made no movement. He only listened, watched. He had two men in or around that depot, one of them wounded, both armed and dangerous. The man who moved first might be the man to die.

Shell had no intention of dying, not just yet. He searched the open area toward the old depot, seeing nothing, no one. What had happened to Frank Tyler? Possibly the young marshal had been tagged. And Jack? Jack was not shot, yet he was holding his ground; probably Riley, the skilled fighter that he was realized that the last thing Shelter needed was a man bursting out of the shadows—not knowing until it was too late if it was a man who had come to help or to kill.

It came then—a scratching sound, low, almost inaudible. It could have been the muffled meeting of boot leather and platform. There was only the one sound, however, and then no more.

Shelter's instincts told him to stay put, to wait out a mistake by Chambers or Weese, yet he also recognized that they might have slipped away, might be making their run while Shell did nothing, and so he moved.

Like a cat creeping through the night, Shelter slid down the board planking of the platform, his eyes going to the dark windows of the depot, the silver rails beyond. Something had disturbed the cattle in the pens to the east; Shelter heard them shift, horns clacking together. One steer bawled against the night.

In the flash of moonlight Shelter saw it—at his feet was a trail of blood, a part of a bootheel imprint smeared in a large drop. His eyes lifted to the closed depot door.

Holding his Colt beside his ear, Shelter nudged the door with a boot toe and it swung open at the broken hasp. Dark inside, it was quiet, deadly. Shell stepped inside in one quick, easy movement, eyes searching the depot's interior.

Moonlight entered the two high windows and glossed the wooden floor, shadowing the wire cage of the ticket office. A freight dolly sat to one side, near a row of wooden benches for passengers.

The trickle of blood was caught in the moonlight. Maroon spots led off toward the back and Shelter eased that way, eyes lifting to the staircase in front of him. Probably there was an attic used for storage up there. That and Luke Weese with a loaded gun.

Shell put a hand on the dark wood of the rail. His toe touched the bottom step and the night ignited with sound and flame. A .44 slug ripped into the wall beside Shelter's head, a second splintered the bannister.

Shelter went to one knee, firing three quick shots through the door above him. Then he rushed forward, boots clicking on the stairs, the staircase filled with rolling smoke.

An answering shot echoed through the depot and Shell ducked low, taking three steps at a time until he was beside the attic door, gasping for breath. Hurriedly he fished in his pockets for his spare cartridges, jamming them into the pistol as quickly as his fingers would work.

The smoke was clearing away slowly, the depot again going to a deathly silence. Weese was in there, or had been—was there a window opening to the outside? Shell had no idea, but if there was Weese, with that shot-up leg would have a hard time making a jump.

The door beside Shelter was badly splintered now, clusters of wooden needles projecting from the bullet holes. It was dark in that room . . . had Weese brought extra ammunition with him? Probably he wore a few loops on his gunbelt—there was no advantage there. Shelter turned it over in his mind every which way, trying to find an edge. He had *one*.

Weese was hurt, bleeding badly from the look of it. By now shock would be setting in, and Weese would know he was trapped, slowly dying. Shell decided to play on that.

"Give it up, Luke. You can't make it. You can hold me off for a time, but you're gaining nothing! You're bleeding to death, man!"

"Shut up, Morgan!" Weese hollered back, hysterically, Shell thought.

"I'm just sayin' it like it is, Luke," Shelter replied. "You can't win. Come morning they'll burn you out . . . if you're still alive, that is."

"I won't hang!" Luke's voice rasped defiantly.

"Who says you will?" Shelter asked mildly. A bullet slammed into the door beside his head and he drew back angrily. That's what a man gets for talking.

"Chambers would see to it," Luke said after a time. His breathing was ragged now. Probably he was trying to bind up that leg, finding whatever he could do to stem the flow of blood would be little enough.

"Chambers?"

"He'd drag us down with him. The son of a bitch is built that way. He'd never go out alone."

"You killed anybody, Luke . . . ?" Shell asked conversationally. "Maybe you won't hang at all." It was silent in the room. There was no answer to that question or to several others. "Luke, you in there? You all right?"

Then Shelter heard a metallic sound, as a hinge might make . . . a hinge! There *was* a window in the attic! He stepped out and drove his boot against the door, banging it open.

Shelter dove into the attic, a low roofed room

filled with trunks and crates. There was a window. The moon beamed through it as Shell came to his feet. High on the wall, it was propped open.

But Weese had not gone through it yet. His damaged leg had forced him to build a platform of trunks to reach the window, and he stood on the trunks now, whirling to face Shelter Morgan, his face white in the moonlight, the flame from his gun red, piercing as Luke Weese pulled the trigger of his pistol.

The bullet whipped past, so close that Shell felt his hair lift, and slammed into the wall behind, but Weese had had his last chance.

Shelter's Colt had come up as Weese fired and now he fired, the .44 slug tearing a gaping hole in Luke Weese's throat. The gunman twitched, dropped his gun and staggered back, toppling through the window at his back to the depot roof. He hit the roof hard, bounced and then rolled off onto the empty tracks before the depot, Shelter Morgan watching him from the window.

Weese did not move, his body twisted crazily. The blood on the window sill was still warm, the attic cold. Shelter holstered his Colt and climbed out onto the roof.

There was a second man out there to be had, and Shelter meant to have him on this night. To have him for Welton Williams, for Dink and Jeb Thornton, for Swede and the Navajo whose name Shell had never gotten.

Shell crouched low and circled the sloped roof. Above him an ornamental turret cut a dark silhouette against the sky. Strawberry, across the way was still quiet. Frost slicked the shingles under Shelter's feet and he paused, searching the empty freight yards for a single sign of movement.

He perched on the edge of the roof momentarily, probing the night, and then his patience was rewarded. A steer in the cattle pens jumped sideways and kicked up his heels, nudging those cattle next to him. Shelter smiled slowly.

Easing to the very edge of the roof he spotted the freight wagon below him and he jumped, landing in the bed of the iron wheeled wagon. Silently he slipped out of the wagon bed, moving across the station platform toward the rails. Beyond them the cattle still milled uneasily.

The moon was bright on the silver rails as Shelter darted across the cinderbed of the rails, stopping beside the water tower, gun held high as he craned his neck toward the stock pens, the open faced hay barn on the far side.

It was cold, Shelter's muscles tight as he crept forward, slipping under a rail into the pen.

The cattle were packed close, their body heat, their scent pervasive as Shell eased around the perimeter of the corral, nudging a brindle steer from his path. Reluctantly the steer moved, but silently. There was no sign of Chambers.

He was in there somewhere, but where?

A nearly white longhorn, rangy, lean walked toward the center of the pen, tail twitching and Shell slid in beside the steer's shoulder, using the longhorn as a shield as he crossed the pen.

A steer bawled near the barn, and Shell saw a flash of silver. Moonlight on metal. He lifted up,

Colt in hand but the gleaming bit of metal had disappeared again, as quickly as it had appeared.

Still, he had an idea now where Chambers was. Shelter abandoned his longhorn bodyguard and eased forward, his hand going to the haunch of a steer which lifted its head lazily and stepped aside.

The hay barn painted a dark shadow across that side of the pens, and it was there that Chambers must be, moving toward the barn.

Shelter drew back the hammer of his Colt, the click loud, unmistakable in the night. The moon had been screened behind the clouds, and now again it broke free, bathing the pens in silver light, and as it did Wes Chambers popped up almost directly in front of Shell.

Chambers fired across the back of a steer, his exploding shot sending the cattle into panicked motion. Shell felt a searing pain high on his shoulder, and he shot back, desperately.

But Chambers was gone, vanishing among the tons of moving cattle. Shell clutched at his shoulder, side-stepped a steer and ducked low.

Wes Chambers was there again, and he fired wildly, the roll of shots churning up the cattle. A steer's shoulder slammed into Shell, levelling him and he went down among the deadly hooves of the cattle.

Shell narrowly missed being stomped by a big red steer, which wide-eyed charged across the pen; and with cold panic Shell realized his gun was gone.

Frantically he searched the earth, dodging a steer, shoving another aside. Their horns clacked together as they milled uneasily, bawling at the tops of their lungs. The Colt was gone! Trampled into the sodden earth, perhaps, or kicked aside.

Slowly Shelter eased toward the rails of the cattle yard, knowing that it had only been luck which kept him from being trampled. Some of those cows carried a thousand pounds of beef on their lanky frames. A hoof would drive right through a man.

If Chambers fired again the panic might be more wide spread, deadly. Of course, Shelter considered wryly, if Chambers fired again Shelter might never know what the result of that shot was.

He only hoped that Wes believed him still armed. If Chambers, wolf that he was, scented death, he would be all over Shell.

Shelter was at the rails now, and he climbed through toward the hay barn. He saw a movement, a shadowy form, he thought, but he could not be sure.

He eased toward the hay barn, letting the shadows from the structure close behind him. Shell's arm was throbbing, his back was bruised from the collision with a steer. Angry with himself for having lost his pistol, he sagged back on the baled hay and ripped open his shirt, examining the bullet wound which was jagged but not deep despite the blood which soaked his shirt sleeve.

"If that one won't do you, I've got more," Wes Chambers said.

Shell looked up slowly. Chambers' face was savage in the moonlight. He held a big blue Colt in his left hand. "I've never seen a man come huntin' death so far and so hard," Chambers panted. He was hunched forward at the shoulders, his arms dangling. "You've chased it, you've found it, Morgan."

Chambers' gun came up and his thumb pulled back the hammer. The moon illuminated a savage grin on his wolfish features.

Then it happened, so suddenly that Shelter could not follow it, comprehend it. Chambers' arm went up and he went to the ground hard, another shadow was on top of him, mauling him like a savage cat. Shell saw a flash of silver, heard Wes Chambers' moan with pain.

Then the man with the knife stood, facing Shelter as Wes Chambers lay dead in a pool of blood.

Banquero!

The Apache tossed his head proudly, clearing the long raven hair from his dark eyes.

"Banquero, I . . ." Shell stood but the Apache only stared at him. Then he walked a few paces away, returning with something heavy, dark in his hand.

He threw it at the feet of Shelter Morgan where it lay like a black iron snake. Banquero's leg irons, dark against the moonlit earth.

"I appreciate it," Shelter said, but Banquero did not answer. His lips twisted into a proud smirk and he shoved his knife back into its sheath. "Banquero?"

The Apache turned on his heel and was gone, slipping into the shadows of the night. After a time Shelter heard the pounding of a horse's hooves, moving away into the desert beyond Strawberry.

Shelter sagged back against the hay. Jack Riley rushed up to him, rifle in his big hand. He took it all in at a glance, Chambers lying dead, Shell's wounded arm. Riley's eyes lifted to the east where Banquero had ridden.

"Wasn't that . . . ?"

"It was Banquero," Shell said.

"Now what the hell . . . ?" Riley pushed back his hat and rubbed his forehead, looking around the barn and again toward the desert.

"I guess it means I'm even," Shelter said. His eyes went to the unmoving form of Wes Chambers. "All around."

17.

It was pleasant, quiet in the bed at Mrs. Dawkins house. Shell shifted slightly, feeling a jab of pain in his arm. He grimaced, yawned and turned back the other way. The sheets were clean, freshly ironed and when someone opened the door to the bedroom a golden morning light patched the walls.

Someone opened the door—Shell opened a lazy eye to see Sylvia standing there in a yellow silk dress, her hair pinned up.

"Good morning," Sylvia said. Her full lips were decorated with a rich smile. Shell sat up, holding his bandaged shoulder immobile as he adjusted his pillow behind his back.

Sylvia's eyes were bright, teasing. She let her gaze run across Shell's hard muscled, bare chest, those cable strung shoulders. She pressed the door shut behind her and turned the key in the lock.

Then, still smiling, she reached behind her and unzipped her dress, letting it fall to the floor. Shell smiled appreciatively, but he asked, "Think this is the time and place for it?"

"I thought it was any time or place with you," Sylvia said coyly. She unpinned her hair, shaking it free so that it fell across her shoulders, full breasts. "I had a taste of you, Mister Morgan. Now I want the full course."

Sitting on the chair she unbuttoned her boots and slowly unrolled her stockings, Shell catching a tantalizing glimpse of the dark shadow between her white thighs.

"What about Mrs. Dawkins?" Shell asked.

"She went to work at her restaurant," Sylvia said. Reaching behind her again she unhooked her corset, her milk-white breasts falling free as it dropped to the floor.

"Penny . . . Frank?" Shell asked, his eyes devouring those full upthrust breasts, the pink nipples.

"They've gone out riding together," Sylvia said. She stepped from the pile of clothing, utterly naked, utterly feminine, her long legs firm, her hips fluid, compelling.

She sat on the bed beside Shell, her face turned away, and Shell ran a finger down her spine, letting his hand caress those ivory hips, slip around to her thigh where his fingertip brushed the downy soft hair between her legs.

"Jack?" Shell asked. Sylvia, her eyes distant. looked back at him, hardly understanding the question. "Where's Jack Riley?"

"He got itchy," Sylvia said. "He told us to apologize to you, but he had to ride. He got a look at Strawberry's jail, I guess, and didn't like it."

"Then there's no one around?"

"No one. Just me . . ." Sylvia bent her head around toward his and her full lips parted, finding Shelter's mouth. "Just me." She stood and pulled back the sheet, slipping in beside Shelter, her body warm, soft.

She came to him hungrily, her mouth against his lips, his throat, his chest. Her hands slid down his long, hard thighs finding Shelter ready as she touched his erection, a tiny sigh of delight escaping from her lips. She buried her face against Shell's chest, her fingers gently stroking his shaft, then dipping between his legs to brush his scrotum, thrilled by the size of the man, the animal scent about him, the utter hardness of his flesh.

Sylvia shifted slightly, sliding her long leg up across Shell's thigh. He grimaced with momentary pain and she kissed his chin lightly, with concern.

"Your shoulder!"

"That's all right," Shell grinned. "It's of little concern right now."

"I don't want you to hurt yourself." Sylvia threw the sheet off, her eyes searching Shell's body, wanting him. "I'll take care of it all," Sylvia said, her eyes sparkling, deep.

"Think you can handle it by yourself?" Shell asked.

"I can . . ." Her lips went to Shelter's chest, slid to his abdomen while her soft palms stroked the inside of his thighs where dark soft hair grew.

She kissed his thighs then, first one then the other,

her hand cradling his erection, and Shell lay back, closing his eyes, letting the sensual luxury of Sylvia's lips and hands envelop him.

Sylvia straddled Shell's thighs, her hands running along his slim hips as she eased slowly forward, watching with hungry fascination as Shell's erection throbbed, and grew still larger, the head of it deep red, calling to her body which responded with a trickle of hot juices. Sylvia shuddered, moving astride of his cock, her fingers spreading her warm lips, simultaneously stroking Shell.

His hands had slipped between her legs as well, finding her clitoris which was taut, swelling. Tantalizingly he stroked it with his rough fingers and Sylvia trembled.

"My God, Morgan!" Sylvia whispered. "I can't . . ." her thighs had begun to tremble, her body to open to the coming delight. Sylvia lifted her hips and grabbed for Shell's shaft, teasing herself with the head of it momentarily before slowly settling onto it, her body heat bringing the pulsing need in Shelter's loins to a frenzy.

"Can you handle it?" Shell asked with a teasing smile and Sylvia nodded, her long dark hair falling across Shell's abdomen as she bent forward, watching Shell enter her with animal fascination.

"Yes . . . I can." Her answer came in puffs of speech as the hunger deep within her rose.

"Then do it, darlin'," Shell told her. "Do it."

Shelter's hands had circled to Sylvia's firm, full hips and he felt the muscles there quiver, felt her slowly lift her body then settle again. Now she lifted herself high so that only the sensitive, needful head of Shell's cock was inserted in her warm cavity, then shuddering, she drove herself downward, taking it all the way in for the first time, her pelvis driving against Shell's.

Sylvia's head came to Shell's, her supple mouth finding his, her breasts just grazing Shell's chest as she swayed forward and back, stroking Shell.

Shell's hand found her breasts, tracing tiny whorl patterns around her nipples, and Sylvia moaned in response. His hands slipped down her smooth sides, finding her quivering hips; and slipping in behind her, his hands spread her still wider, finding the sweet juices of her body there.

Sylvia threw her head back, her eyes distant, unfocused, and she methodically swayed up and then back, slowly letting Shell's erection penetrate her deeply before drawing forward, holding him just inside.

Suddenly she quivered and her lips began to move more rhythmically, Shell clenching her buttocks roughly as she built to a frantic pace, her head rolling from side to side as the intensity built. She arched her neck high, let out a moan of deep delight then buried her face against Shelter's chest as she thrust against Shell, bringing his trembling need to a hot rushing climax.

Shell held her white buttocks savagely, the tendons in his throat standing taut as he pulled himself into Sylvia, feeling her warmth flooding over him, the trembling inside of her, the animal bites she applied to his throat, chin, cheek as he came, quaking, deeply.

They lay together silently a long while, Sylvia on

top of him, her fingers stroking his thighs, shoulders, her soft breasts against his chest, her tiny kisses finding his ears, eyes as her heart slowed from its dreadful pounding.

She lay silently next to him, but Shell could feel the movements deep inside of her. Rolling, fluid waves and she whispered to Shell, "Don't move. Don't move. I'm coming again, but oh, God, Shell, don't move! It's so nice this way."

She squealed suddenly, a shrill, utterly joyful sound and her full mouth kissed Shell's once deeply, her hips and abdomen rippling with pleasure.

Silently they lay together then, the morning passing in peaceful moments. After a while Sylvia sat up, her hips still across Shell's abdomen, her dark hair in a tangle across her breasts, her shoulders.

"I told you I could handle it alone," she said.

"It was a good start," Morgan answered, feigning a yawn. Sylvia scowled good-naturedly, her hands against Shell's chest, her finger toying with his small nipple.

"How's your shoulder?" she asked.

"Feelin' better. Like the rest of me," Shell answered with a nod. "Thanks to you."

"You need a massage," Sylvia announced, climbing off of Shell, letting his cock fall free. She let her hand linger lovingly on it, feeling her own warm juices there.

"I do?" Shell lifted one lazy eyelid. "Well that's somethin'. And here I thought I was plenty relaxed already."

"Doesn't seem you're *that* relaxed," Sylvia said, squeezing him playfully. "Anyway," she said, wiping the hair back from her face, "the massage is for your backside. *That* hasn't seen much exercise for a time. Your muscles will wither away."

"Hope not!" Shell grinned. Sylvia's eyes were still on his crotch and she answered,

"Not that one. I don't think I could beat it to death with a stick."

"Just promise me you won't try," Morgan said. "Well, I guess if you're going to play nurse, I've got to play patient." He rolled over gingerly, protecting the gunshot shoulder.

Sylvia straddled him again, and Shell closed his eyes enjoying the kneading fingers she worked against his back muscles, the feel of her still dewy, warm crotch against his buttocks as she shifted across him, humming as she worked.

"I think you got a knack for that," Shell said, his voice muffled by the pillow.

"Do you?"

"Definitely."

Sylvia slid back down Shell's thighs, her hands going to his lower back, his hard muscled buttocks. Playfully she leaned forward and nipped him on the ass and Shell's head came around with a start.

"I couldn't resist it," Sylvia said.

"Never heard of no nurse doing that," Shell grumbled.

Sylvia leaned forward again and kissed him where her teeth marks still showed. Her fingers ran around his buttocks, toying with the fine dark hair at the base of his spine. Then her hand dropped between Shelter's legs and she sighed pleasurably, finding the prize.

"Nurses don't do that either . . . none that I've run across," Shell told her.

"They must. If you were their patient, Shell, they damn sure would." Her thumb and forefinger encircled the head of his half erect cock and she lovingly ministered to it, watching it swell, change to a warm color and unbend with anticipation.

"That's about enough of that," Shell said.

"Oh?"

"Just enough." Shell rolled over and gently he lay Sylvia on the bed beside him. "That's enough playin' nurse, and enough of you doin' all the doin'," he said, leaning to her to find her mouth in a longing kiss. Her hands went to his shoulders as Shell's fingers dropped to her crotch, finding her ready, eager again.

Shell sat up, facing away from Sylvia who stroked his strong back, her breasts rising and falling heavily as Shell's fingers gently opened the pink rose between Sylvia's legs, stroking each tender petal, touching the nectar there.

"Oh, God, Shell!" Sylvia said, her voice low, guttural, "I don't need any massaging. Just fuck me. Please."

"That's about what I had in mind," Shell said, rolling on top of her, grinning that little boy grin. He kissed her lips, the nape of her neck, going to her nipples which were pink, taut. He suckled there for a while, going from one to the other.

"You promised," Sylvia said, her fingers clenching Shelter's back. Her knees had come up and she spread them wide apart.

"Promised what?" Shelter teased.

She breathed it into his ear, biting at the lobe. "Fuck me, Shelter. I can't wait."

Shell scooted down a little bit, his erection sliding naturally between her white thighs, finding the warm, beckoning haven there of its own accord.

Sylvia pulled him to her, her hands clawing at his shoulders, her mouth tearing at his as Shelter drove it in to the hilt, Sylvia gasping as it hit home.

There was no waiting then. Shelter began to rock against her pelvis, moving in a circular motion, finding every nerve ending, every pinpoint of pleasure within Sylvia.

Her upper lip was beaded with perspiration jewels, her lips were parted, and she rolled her head to one side then the other, beginning a frantic thrusting of her own, her knees drawn up nearly to her quivering breasts as she tried to meet Shelter's body with every part of her own.

She swayed and rolled, her hands going to Shell's buttocks, digging at them as if she would draw the whole man inside of her where her body ached for more and still more.

He was hard, deep within her, touching every inch of her with his magic wand, and the rippling built up in Sylvia, the swelling which built until it seemed it would burst, and then it did burst, sending a shuddering wave of joyous release sweeping across her thighs, pelvis, going to her breasts as she came completely undone, her mouth sucking savagely at Shelter Morgan who still was not done.

He arched his back and thrust against her, taking deep, slow strokes, lifting her hips still higher with one hand as he centered himself, finding the target of delight which he stroked again until Sylvia thought she would go mad. With a furious, sobbing climax she rolled her hips madly, wanting all of him, more than all.

Tenderly she glanced up, seeing him, every muscle tense, shoulders, abdomen, thighs and her hands went to his cock plunged deep within her.

"Come," she whispered. And she moved her silky hips slowly, touching him everywhere, her eyes and Shelter's meeting. Then he grinned, sunk it to the hilt and came. Deeply, satisfyingly, and Sylvia stroked him, feeling him pulse within her, feeling the tension leak out of his beautiful, hard body.

Together they lay in the bed through the morning and into the afternoon, napping or caressing one another, Sylvia making small sounds of comfort, like a cat's purring when she snuggled next to Shelter or turned, pressing her buttocks out to contact him.

Shell stroked her hair, kissed the center of her back and said, "It's getting on." By the shadows he could tell that evening was not far off. Mrs. Dawkins would be returning, Frank and Penny.

"I don't want to get up," Sylvia pouted. She swept back her black hair and kissed Shell. His hands momentarily cupped her full, pendulous breasts.

"I know it."

Reluctantly she slid from the bed, dressing slowly, her eyes still on Shelter's naked body. "You'd better pull that sheet up," Sylvia said with mock sternness. "If Penny comes back to find you like that . . ."

It was a joke, but Shelter could read the hint of uneasiness that lay behind the remark. He tried to defuse it. "Or Mrs. Dawkins, maybe," he laughed.

"I wouldn't even doubt that—God, Shelter, you're beautiful, don't you know that?"

"Dress," he said roughly, closing his eyes to end the conversation. After a minute he heard the whisper of skirts and felt Sylvia's lips brush his as she bent low over him, her dark eyes searching his face.

"Better scoot," Shell said. She nodded slowly and he hooked a hand behind her neck, drawing her to him for one last, lingering kiss.

"What will happen now?" Sylvia wanted to know. Sitting up in bed, Shelter smiled in response to her worried expression.

"When my arm's better?"

"Yes."

"There's a man I need to find, Sylvia—you know that. There's a man in Steamboat who chains men up like animals and sells them to the highest bidder. A man who turned his back on his own kind, murdered them for gold.

"A man," Shelter said quietly, watching Sylvia's face, "I trusted more than any man on earth. I fought with him, went hungry with him, suffered with Fainer. Then he came at me with a gun, Sylvia. He cheated me, lied to me, killed other men—my men. Those who trusted the both of us."

"You'll ride to Steamboat," she said with frustration.

"That's it."

"To fight again, to walk into another bullet!" Sylvia was going to add more, but she could read the dark

212

resolve in Shelter Morgan's eyes and she knew that arguing with the man could only drive him away from her.

"I'll come with you," Sylvia said.

"You will not!" Shelter shook his head. "You don't need to see it . . . whatever happens, and I don't want the worry of you on my mind."

"Then later," she pleaded, coming nearer to Shelter, her hands twisting one another with emotion. "I could come to Steamboat in a few days, couldn't I . . . Shell?"

"In a few days," he agreed reluctantly, and Sylvia's face brightened instantly. "I don't know how you'll find me."

"That's the easy part, Shelter Morgan," Sylvia said, kissing him lightly once more before unlocking the door to his bedroom. "I'll just look for a crowd of women, and I'll march over and pull you out of the middle of them."

After Sylvia was gone Shelter dressed slowly, careful not to tear that shoulder loose again. He heard horses out in the yard and when he came out minutes later Frank and Penny Dolittle were coming in the front door, laughing, Frank's arm around Penny's waist.

"Shelter!" Frank looked up, flushing deeply. His arm dropped from Penny's waist. Shell, leaning against the door jamb smiled in amusement.

Frank Tyler crossed the room and stood before Shelter, and the kid's eyes were sober, his forehead furrowed. "I've got to talk to you," Tyler said.

"Sure." Shell shrugged, his eyes lifting to Penny. He finished tucking in his shirt. "Go ahead."

"Not here . . ." Frank looked around, meeting Penny's gaze.

Penny came forward, her hair, in ringlets, swaying perkily. Shelter had never seen her fixed up like this, and she looked fine. In a new calico dress, there was a hint of perfume about her.

"No, Frank," Penny said. "I'll talk to Shelter."

Frank started to object, but did not. Shell's eyes went from one of them to the other. Neither was willing to meet his gaze.

"Outside," Penny said. Then she turned sharply on her heel, marching toward the front door, her slim back straight, purposeful. Shell followed, shutting the door behind him.

Outside it was cool, a few high flags of cloud across the late afternoon sky. A dog barked in uptown Strawberry. Penny leaned back against the trunk of the big oak in Mrs. Dawkin's yard. It was a time before she found the words she wanted.

"We didn't want to hurt you," Penny said softly, her brown eyes wide. She looked down abruptly.

"No?" Shelter suppressed a smile. He waited for Penny to continue.

"I know after what you and I went through . . . you naturally thought . . . I thought, and I told Frank," she stammered.

"Are you going to tell *me?*" Shell asked.

"I don't want to hurt you," Penny repeated.

"I don't want to be hurt."

"It's over between us, Shell," she blurted out. "Frank and I are going to be married when he gets back from Steamboat. He thinks he'll run for sheriff here in Strawberry."

"You and Frank . . ." Shell carefully kept his poker face on.

"I'm sorry."

"I know," he said quietly. He could not help a tiny smile as he studied the peppery, tiny girl before him. "Well, I'm glad then." He added, "If it has to be that way."

"It does," she said stiffly, sniffing.

"Well, there's nothin' to say," Shelter said, toeing the earth underfoot, "but good luck. I wish you the best."

"Oh, thank you, Shelter!" She got on tip-toes and kissed him. "I knew you'd understand."

"It ain't easy," Shell told her, rubbing his jaw.

"You see, I'm not a poor girl anymore. Zukor made his run, and Frank says that Earl Weese will testify that Chambers and Zukor killed my parents then stole that property. Why, I'll be practically wealthy!"

"You'll be too good for me," Shell agreed.

"Now you know I didn't mean that," Penny said softly. She touched his cheek with her small hand. "I'll never forget what you did, what we had. But Frank's my man, and that's all there is to it."

"Then good luck, I know it will work," Shelter said.

Penny reached up to kiss him again, then she hoisted her skirts and ran back toward the house where Frank waited in the doorway. Shelter turned away toward the fading evening skies, hiding the grin on his face.

18.

Shelter had kicked his chair back from the dinner table, and sitting there watching the fire twist into golden patterns, he smoked his first cigar in a long time. Mrs. Dawkins and Penny pattered around the kitchen, their voices low, confidential. Shell picked up a word now and then—most of it about china and lace and such—but he hardly paid attention to it.

His thoughts were elsewhere—on Sylvia who had taken a room at the hotel, and on Fainer who was waiting in Steamboat. At least he had been there, and that worried Shelter. Things were going too slowly; there was a chance Fainer had gotten word about what had happened in Strawberry and was even now lighting out for new territory.

But Shelter had promised Frank Tyler to sit tight, to wait until things could be done legally and proper. And so he had waited, waited three long days. The draft from the opening door whipped the fire in the hearth and Shelter lifted his eyes, cigar clenched between his teeth.

Frank Tyler stood there in a top coat and hat. He crossed the room to where Shelter sat. Then, with a grin, Tyler slapped the packet of papers he carried down on the table.

"What's that?" Shell asked, lifting an eyebrow.

"What you've been waiting for," Frank said, tilting back his hat as he sat across the table from Shell, "warrants for Judge Fainer's arrest."

Shelter let the legs of his chair slap to the floor as he leaned forward, untying the ribbon around the heavy parchment on which the warrants were written.

He read them slowly, the cigar smoke curling past his lean dark face as he squinted at the documents by the firelight. "There's a whole lot of whereases and wherefores in here, Frank. What's it mean? What have we got him for?"

"Trafficking in slaves, dereliction of duty, using his office for profit, graft and bribery, failing to execute the decision of a lawful court . . ." Frank counted on his fingers.

"Hold it! Hold it!" Shell laughed, holding his hands up. "What I want to know," he asked, his voice growing serious again, "is, will Fainer hang if we catch him?"

"Hang?" Frank Tyler studied the strong face of the man across the table from him, the fire in Morgan's blue-gray eyes, the cigar burning in his hand. "No, Shelter, he won't hang. But if he's convicted on even half of these counts," Frank tapped the warrants, "and he *will* be, he'll spend the rest of his natural life in prison."

Shell nodded thoughtfully. "I guess I'll have to settle for that." Then he stood, "Excuse me."

"Where are you going?" Tyler asked.

"To pack my roll," Shelter replied. "We're riding, aren't we?"

"Yes. We're riding." Frank hesitated. "Before you go—there's something else here."

"Oh?" Shelter turned, his eyes narrowing. Frank Tyler had placed a marshal's badge on the table and he shoved it toward Shell.

"I commissioned this for you, Shell. You ever wore one?"

"Never had the urge," Shelter said evenly. He added, "I don't have the urge now."

"Take it anyway," Frank encouraged him, "it might keep you out of a lot of trouble."

"I've met a lot of lawmen who wouldn't subscribe to that theory," Shell commented. Nevertheless he picked up the star and shoved it in his pocket, mostly for Frank's sake.

Frank Tyler might accomplish a lot, given time, but it would always be by the book. Still, a marshal carrying warrants and a badge would be protected by the law if it came to shooting, and Shelter gave in.

"Better say your goodbyes, Frank," Shelter said, nodding toward the kitchen. "When I've got my roll packed, I mean to be riding. If you want to be there when it starts, best move quickly yourself."

Frank's lips compressed momentarily with pique—just who the hell did Morgan think was running this show! Then, watching the tall man disappear into the bedroom, Frank smiled.

Shelter Morgan, that's who, and Frank Tyler knew it.

He sighed, planted his palms flat on the table and rose, going to the warm kitchen where Penny, dish towel in hand, turned to meet him.

They rode out that night with a white moon shining on the long trail before them, the shadows deep in the cold, barren canyons.

Shelter was riding a deep-chested buckskin horse with a black mane and tail. A good running horse, it was purchased for him by Frank Tyler. Being a deputy marshal did have some advantages, Shelter had to admit. It was the finest horse he had straddled in a long while, minding a light touch on the reins, moving with a long, land-devouring stride which was smooth enough to make the riding pleasurable.

They camped along Cottonwood Wash, up along a rocky feeder gorge. Castle Butte cut a stark silhouette against the western sky. It was silent, cool along the wash.

The fire flickered low as Frank Tyler boiled coffee for them. There was a wind fussing in the canyons, toying with the fire, but the world was empty, both below and above where the stars clustered around that white moon, and Shell found it peaceful being there. He said so to Frank.

"It is. I think maybe it's because we have a

primitive memory of living like this within us. Nomads, solitary people whose greatest joy was warmth, food, a fire." Tyler was silent, his own eyes going to the distances.

"Look at that," Shell complained. He had pulled off his boot and the scars from the leg irons were still plainly evident. "Be a long time before I forget Zukor, Chambers and them. *That* will be there to remind me."

"Did Penny tell you that Zukor made a run for it?" Frank asked over a scalding cup of coffee.

"She did," Shell nodded.

"He didn't get far. I didn't tell Penny all of the story.".

"Oh?" Shelter's blue eyes lifted questioningly to the young marshal.

"They found him out along Washboard Creek," Frank told him in a low voice. "He was dead. Murdered. His neck was broken, Shelter, his head twisted nearly off his body."

"That's something," Shell said, "but I guess he had it coming."

"I guess so," Frank said.

"Hell of a way to go, though," Shelter said, leaning back. He lay still for a moment and then unrolled his bed, smoothing out the ground underneath. Neither of them said another word about Zukor's death, conjectured on it, the way it was done.

But Shelter had always thought it was funny the way Jack Riley pulled out without saying a word to anybody.

They rode out at dawn, the deep rose and amber

hues of the canyons rapidly fading to brilliant white beneath the glare of the Arizona sun.

Frank Tyler's face was coated with dust, his eyebrows frosted with it by midday when he eased the blue roan he rode over next to Shelter's buckskin.

"We'll hit Steamboat in the morning," Tyler commented.

"With luck."

"Any idea on how we're going to handle this?" Tyler asked cautiously.

"The easy way. We'll ask him to come along." Tyler seemed relieved by the response and he grinned. It was a short-lived expression of happiness, however, when Shell added, "Of course he won't come along quietly."

"There's a chance . . ."

"A chance," Shell agreed. If Fainer was eager to spend the rest of his life in a Federal prison. Knowing Fainer, Shell doubted it. "He won't be alone, you know?"

Frank blinked at Shell, wiping the perspiration from his eyes. *That*, for some reason had not occurred to the young marshal.

"But surely . . . why, he couldn't know . . ." But Fainer could very easily know.

"Even if he don't," Shell commented. "Men like this have people around them. Insurance guns, you might say. Beats the hell out of bein' hung."

Frank Tyler rode silently for a time, his head bowed thoughtfully. Finally as they let the horses drink at a creek crossing he asked Shelter, "Then you're expecting a shooting arrest?"

"Not exactly," Shell had to tell him. "Frank, I'm expecting a war." He swung back into the buckskin's saddle, "I'm thinkin' we'd better be ready for it."

The afternoon passed slowly. A dry, arid stretch of land lay between them and Steamboat. They had seen the last water they would see. Frank Tyler rode silently, and Shelter knew what was on his mind.

A young fellow, wanting to get married, settle down, he was going to spend the morning in an armed struggle.

"You ever think you might be in the wrong business, Frank?" Shelter asked him quietly once.

"Yes," he replied soberly. "I've thought of that. But it's a little late for resigning now, isn't it?"

They camped with the lights of Steamboat in sight on that evening, the hurried rush of color produced by the sunset flooding out briefly across the desert before that light faded and the bone white moon dominated the desert night.

They made no fire, boiled no coffee. Shell silently munched on a dry ham sandwich Mrs. Dawkins had packed hurriedly. The night was much the same as the night before—the starlit night which had inspired a poetic vein in Frank Tyler, quiet appreciation in Shelter. But this night, identical as it was, inspired only thoughts of death. The wind seemed colder, the ground harder as Shell rolled out his bed.

He sat for some time, checking the mechanisms on his weapons by the pale moonlight, counting rounds of ammunition before turning in.

He could see Frank Tyler's eyes, open in the starlight as the kid searched the skies, thinking the thoughts a man thinks on a night which may be his last on earth.

19.

Steamboat wasn't much as towns go, smaller than Strawberry even. In the early days it had been a trading post, and the post had grown when the Territorial government decided to make it the county seat. The railroad, however, had never come to Steamboat, nor any industry of any kind.

There was only one building along the main drag which was not of raw adobe construction. The courthouse which had been built to last, of red brick and iron reinforcing. It was a shame the justice had not lasted as long as the building.

At midday the long, dark man on the buckskin pony and the kid on the blue roan trailed into Steamboat, their eyes sweeping the dusty main street, going to the shadows, the rooftops. There was no point in delaying it, so Shelter led Frank Tyler directly to the courthouse, where they swung down, Shelter slipping his Winchester from the scabbard.

Frank's face was grim, his hands clenched as they strode up the white steps. Shelter, out of habit, glanced over his shoulder, seeing no one.

Inside it was cool, dark. Their bootheels clicked on the wooden floor as they walked the long corridor, eyes going to the signs above the various doors.

A clerk in shirt-sleeves and spectacles glanced up nervously from the sheaf of papers in his hands as the two men passed.

"Here."

Frank Tyler had pulled up short, his eyes going to the gilt lettering on the door, then back to the cool, confident man who stood with him, Winchester glittering in his hands. Shelter looked twice at the door. So it was time—

"Judge Fainer," Shelter read out loud, the name in front of his eyes jogging many memories to life. Bloody memories. "Open it up!" Shelter said suddenly, sharply.

Frank hesitated, his hand on the brass knob. Then he turned it slowly, and the door swung open, Shelter Morgan stepping into the doorway, his Winchester ready.

The man in the black robe sat behind the big mahogany desk, a pen in hand, and for the first time Frank Tyler drew his pistol, taking a step into the room.

"No, Frank," Shelter said, putting a hand on Tyler's wrist. The man was not Fainer.

"Sir?" the judge, a man with receding white hair and an oversized nose glanced up.

"Marshal Frank Tyler; my deputy," the kid nodded.

"I see." The judge lifted an eyebrow studying the guns in their hands. "I've seen some over anxious lawmen in my time . . . what is it you want?" he demanded.

"Judge Fainer," Frank Tyler told him. "We've warrants on the man and the sign on the door identified it as his office."

"I see." The judge nodded, fixing his eyes on Frank who sheepishly holstered his pistol. "There simply hasn't been time to change the sign. I'm Judge Tabor Fields, Fainer's successor."

"And where's Fainer?" Shelter asked.

Fields lifted his eyes to the deputy, not liking the hard cut of the man's face, those penetrating, cold blue eyes.

"Dead," he responded.

"Dead?" Shelter frowned, exchanged a glance with Frank Tyler and asked the judge, "When?"

"A week ago yesterday," Fields said. The judge stood, rolling up the long, flared sleeves of his robe. He circled the desk and stood before the window, staring out at the squat adobe town, the white, rolling desert beyond Steamboat. "Apparently Judge

Fainer wasn't much of a judge," Fields said. He turned and eyed the warrants Frank still held, "but then, you know that already."

"What happened?" Frank asked. He seemed relieved by this turn of events. Shelter, on the other hand, was only frustrated. Oddly, there was still a portrait of Fainer, in robes, law book in his hands on the wall, looking quite grave, upstanding.

"One might say his own brand of justice was visited upon him," Fields said with a faint shrug. "He had tried a man named Weber Jackson, a poor dirt farmer and sentenced him to hang for murder —the trial was a Swiss cheese of omissions, distortions, heavy-handedness. Yet Jackson was found guilty, and hung.

"One week later the Widow Jackson visited the judge, and in her skirts she had concealed a huge old Walker Colt. Five times she got him, Marshal. The one shot that missed . . ." Fields walked behind his desk and pointed at the hole in the wall there.

As they walked from the office, Frank commented to Shelter, "It was justice, really. Fainer had done terrible things under the name of the law. Many of them matters he could not have been tried for. And now," Tyler said, putting a hand on Shelter's shoulder, "it's over."

"Now it's going to be tougher," Shelter said. Frank looked at him oddly, but said nothing else until they had gone out the front door of the courthouse into the brilliant sun.

"What did you mean by that?" Frank asked. "You got what you wanted—Fainer's dead."

226

"I ain't seen the body," Shelter said. Slowly he swung into the saddle of the buckskin, Frank Tyler's eyes on the dark man, his set jaw, those eyes which peered out from beneath the shadow of his hat brim into the glare of day.

"You can't think . . ." Tyler glanced around and then stepped into the saddle, following Shelter up the dusty road. "Why are we riding out, in that case?"

"We're giving 'em a little slack," Shelter said. He stopped the horse suddenly and turned sideways in the saddle to face Tyler. "Look, Frank, you can ride on out if you want, ride back to Strawberry and get yourself hitched to that little girl there. I can see you don't have the stomach for this. Willing as you were to believe that judge, to forget all about Fainer."

"It's just that . . ." Tyler began, but Shelter interrupted him.

"As for me, Frank, I won't forget Fainer, none of them. It's more than just a job to me—it's a thing I have to do to go on callin' myself a man. I've got no settle-down life waitin' down the road, or maybe I'd feel different about it. *You* do. Make your choice, Frank. I won't think the lesser of you if you ride on out of Steamboat; you've done your duty. I've still got *mine* to do."

Frank Tyler swallowed hard; momentarily he felt anger stir within him, then a kind of shame. He had to admit that Shelter had it pegged right—he wanted to marry Penny, to live quietly, and not end up face down in some dusty street. He took a deep breath.

It was not easy for Frank but he replied, "I guess I can't say I've done my duty if I ride out. I guess I might have a hard time calling myself a man too. I'm with you, Shell. I want to see that body too."

It was a cute little trick Fields and Fainer had worked up—assuming, of course, that it was a trick—and it might have worked with Tyler alone, or another disinterested marshal.

With Shelter Morgan it was unconvincing. He had the need to be sure. The first step was trying to find the Widow Jackson, which proved impossible. Oddly enough the woman had picked up and gone back east to live with a sister—no one knew exactly where, possibly Indiana.

"Everyone seems convinced the judge is dead," Frank said.

Shell nodded. "Most everybody." But why wouldn't they be? It had happened in the judge's chambers, the woman had admitted to it, been quickly tried and acquitted. Most folks are willing to accept a plausible story repeated often enough. It had been in the newspaper, sworn to in cold print and the court records.

"You're not convinced yet?" Frank asked.

Shelter simply turned those blue-gray eyes on Frank and smiled. "Let's find the judge's house," he suggested.

It was a mile out of the north side of town, up along a creekside road which was lined with silver cottonwoods. A white, two-storied house of some size, the home sat back along a grassy knoll, encircled by a wrought-iron fence.

"Fainer didn't do bad for himself with that

judgin'," Shelter said soberly. There was a slight breeze shifting the leaves of the cottonwoods. "Ready?"

Frank Tyler nodded dubiously, but he followed Shelter across the creek and up the gravel road toward the big white house which seemed silent, empty.

A row of young cypress trees had been planted on the windward side of the house, and off to the north sat a white barn with several sheds clustered around it. Fainer had done well.

"Looks deserted," Frank ventured. Nearer to the house now, they could see that sheets had been hung across the front windows. There was no sign of any activity, but Shell's head came around abruptly. He had heard a distinctive sound, far off along the creek. A horse nickered impatiently and Shell's muscles tensed.

He looked to Frank whose lips were compressed tightly, his pistol now drawn and resting on the saddle. Shell nodded off to the south.

There it sat. A little patch of iron fenced land with a big headstone in the middle of it. Fainer's grave. Shell turned the buckskin that way, his eyes going to the balcony of the house, the barn beyond.

Shell opened the gate to the graveyard without stepping from the buckskin's saddle, nudging his horse on through, he sat for a moment looking at the white monument, the wilted flowers on the freshly turned earth.

"In kind of a hurry, weren't they?" he asked Frank. At the kid's blank expression, Shelter told him, "There's no inscription on the stone."

"What'll we do now?" Frank asked. The wind lifted his fine dark hair as he removed his hat to wipe his brow. He already knew what Shelter's answer would be.

"Now we dig it up," Shell replied. "Let's find us some shovels."

"You know we're breaking the law now," Tyler suggested. "Without a court order . . ."

"Frank," Shelter said with a touch of annoyance, "you sure worry a whole hell of a lot about your warrants and court orders. Tell me—think Judge Fields would have signed a paper allowin' us to dig this up?"

Frank was silent. He knew Morgan was going to do it with or without him, and so he simply followed Morgan back toward the barn. The day was incredibly clear, a lone crow winging through the skies, cawing.

Shelter leaned out of the saddle and tried the door to a small shed, but it was locked. Turning they went to the barn itself. Shell swung down, lifting the wooden bar latch.

Inside it was cool, smelling of hay and horses although there were no longer any horses in the place. He found a tool rack; a pitchfork and a couple of shovels hung there.

Frank was silhouetted in the doorway, still sitting his horse, hands on the pommel as Shelter turned. And as he turned he heard the movement overhead and he spun back, dropping the shovel, his hand flickering toward his Colt.

It was an instant too slow. From the loft above the guns opened up, the bullets slamming into the wall behind Shell as he fired back from the hip, watching as Frank's horse bucked and then took to his heels. He could not tell if Frank had gone down or not. There was no time to ponder it.

A bullet dug up the earth at Shelter's feet and he fired back, punching holes in the floor of the loft. There were at least two men, probably three.

A head lifted and Shell touched off, and the barn filled with the scream of a painfully wounded man. Shelter darted toward cover, crossing the barn in three quick strides, leaping over a bale of hay to duck behind the cover of a stall as bullets dogged his steps, splintered the dark rough planking of the stall, the barn wall beyond.

The back door to the barn swung suddenly open as Shelter crouched behind the stall and Frank Tyler's horse came running in from out of the brilliant light, drawing a hail of gunfire.

But Frank was not on the horse, as the guns turned on the suddenly appearing roan, Tyler ran through the shadows from the front door, landing with a dive beside Shelter as the bullets from the loft peppered the area.

"Not bad," Shelter said with a grin and Frank grinned back.

"Ready to take it to them?" the kid asked. Shelter nodded slowly, soberly.

"I'm ready, Frank. I damn sure am."

Tyler slid along behind the stalls and when he had reached his position, he nodded. Frank fired twice through the floorboards overhead and as he did, Shelter made his move, running to the ladder which ran vertically to the trapdoor of the loft.

Shell took up his position and nodded back to Frank who scrambled back across the barn, drawing an instant reaction from above. A bullet whined off something heavy, metallic, a second tagged Frank and he clutched at his leg as he tumbled into the stall opposite.

But Shelter had seen it all only out of the corner of his eye. There was no time to be a spectator, and as Frank started his run, Shelter climbed the ladder, slamming open the trapdoor to be met by a hand thrusting a Colt into his face.

Reaching out Shelter locked his grip around the gunman's wrist and pulled, hard. The Colt exploded near Shell's face, burning his cheek, forehead with searing black gunpowder, setting his ears to ringing as the gunman, jerked off balance by Shelter's tug, tumbled forward and fell through the empty space below, slamming against the barn floor head first.

The man lay there, his neck broken, gun a few feet from his dead hand, but Shelter did not dwell on it. He took a deep breath, drawing back the hammer on his Colt and then he was up, into the loft, and the thunder guns exploded, all of them aimed at Shelter Morgan.

Shell went to a knee, felt the whiff of passing lead near his cheek and saw a bearded cowboy go down in his sights. The loft echoed and re-echoed with the roar of the guns, a sheet of black powder smoke rolled across the barn, clinging to the ceiling. Suddenly it was silent.

Shelter came slowly to his feet, shakily, his eyes raw, stinging with the gunpowder.

"I should have known it would be you."

"It's me, Colonel," Shelter said. Fainer sat sagged on a bale of hay, gun dangling between his knees as he lifted somber eyes to the tall man before him.

"How has it been, Shell?" Fainer asked.

"It's been a long trail, sir. I've spent some time running, some time finding the others."

"The others?" Fainer glanced wearily at Shelter, as if not understanding.

"Leland Mason, Sergeant Plum, Twyner, Wakefield—Wes Chambers, of course."

"That's quite a list, Captain Morgan," Fainer said, "a long and bloody list."

"Yes, sir. Nearly as bloody as your own."

"What do you mean!" Fainer snapped, coming to life.

"Welton Williams, Dinkum, Jeb Thornton . . . other men you maybe never knew. A Navajo brave, a gambler named Swede . . . your list is long, Colonel. And it was growing longer."

"Yes." Fainer's shoulders hunched with resignation. He looked at the cocked revolver in his hands, then back to Shelter Morgan. "You were a damned good officer, Shell."

"So were you, sir. Once."

"Once." Fainer said it dreamily and then he looked again at Shell, a wan smile crossing his lips. He drew the revolver and Shell flinched, but Fainer had only one intention and as Shell watched the colonel put the muzzle of that .44 to his own temple and pulled off.

The gunshot was loud in the closed barn and Shell grimaced. Fainer, or what had been Fainer, lay smeared against the loft. Turning, gun still dangling from his hand, Shelter looked over to see how Frank had fared.

The marshal was below, clutching his lower leg tightly, but apparently fit. He lifted his eyes to Shelter.

"Is it all right?" Frank called up.

All right?

Shelter turned back to where Fainer lay, dead by his own hand. Was this *all right?* It was simply over. Shell dragged the body to the edge of the loft and let it drop to the barn floor below, Frank Tyler flinching as it thudded inertly against the hard earth.

"Everything's all right, Frank," Shelter waved back. He smiled, but Frank Tyler decided he had never seen a smile with less life in it, less warmth.

He watched as Shelter slowly climbed down the ladder from the loft, watched as Morgan threw Fainer's body across the saddle of his horse and led the buckskin from the barn.

Silently, incredulously, Frank Tyler watched as Shelter led the buckskin through the fading daylight toward the graveyard. Lifting Fainer's body from the uneasy horse's back, Shelter Morgan walked to the grave and lay the colonel down.

He stood there for a moment, silently, then he turned and walked his pony out, closing the gate behind him. "You all right, Frank?" Morgan asked suddenly.

"A little meat shot off my calf," Frank said. "It hurts but I feel better for having it."

"You did what had to be done," Shelter nodded. He helped Frank up behind him on the buckskin and they rode slowly through the deepening shadows toward the creek and Steamboat beyond.

20.

There were a few items to be cleaned up in Steamboat. Fields was locked up, awaiting the arrival of a Territorial Supreme Court judge who would try him and examine the entire situation, making recommendations to see that nothing like this convict labor scheme popped up again.

Those who had escaped from the chain gang, Tex Corson, Torres and Jack Riley, had their sentences commuted, not that it mattered, none of them was ever seen north of the border again. Duncan was shot to death within the month down in Tucson in some sort of bar dispute. Banquero, so they said, was back riding with the renegade Chiricahuas.

Frank Tyler was staying around Steamboat, letting his leg heal up while he waited to give his testimony in the case. They had also put the clamps on Shelter Morgan, wanting him to have his day in court, and it chafed.

There was little to do but lay up in his hotel room, catching up on lost sleep. That and the constant questioning of anyone who might have met up with another member of that traitors' crew from Georgia. He heard little. An old trapper thought he had run across Hugh Whistler who had been a sergeant, high up in the Rockies. A drifting gambler had a notion that General Custis himself was living in San Francisco, but none of it was firm information.

Penny had not yet come up from Steamboat, and Frank was just as happy, wanting his leg to heal up first, so as not to worry the girl—he still had notions of sheriffing in Steamboat and thought that Penny might not be for it so much once she had seen him gunshot.

Steamboat was having its own election for town marshal and for mayor, and there was a novelty to study—they were letting the women vote in Steamboat. They didn't have much choice about it; the women were in the streets with signs and rolling pins, shouting down the hecklers as they pushed one of their own for mayor.

As Shelter pulled his hat on and walked from the

hotel, he was set on by a pack of women with a petition and they virtually encircled him, all shouting at once, shoving the petition and pen at Shelter.

"We want Clarissa Cummings for mayor!" someone shouted.

"Well then I hope you get her," Shelter said, tipping his hat.

Across the street the morning stage had pulled in, and as the dust cleared, Shell saw Frank Tyler embracing Penny Dolittle. They waved to him and he shrugged. Head and shoulders above the women, he was unable to get out of the throng.

"You have to sign this petition," one sharp-voiced woman said loudly.

"I don't live in Steamboat," Shell explained, "I won't be here for the election."

"You have to sign the petition," they argued, listening only to their own voices and not to Shelter's protests. Then beyond them, waiting at the stage depot, Shell saw Sylvia Woods standing, and Shell grabbed the petition.

"Give me that." He smiled at Sylvia and scrawled a signature.

Slowly then he was able to disentangle himself, tipping his hat, nodding, smiling to ladies he had never met, would never see again. They marched off up the street, swooping down on the next un-suspecting victim.

Shell strode the dusty street, dodging a freight wagon. Sylvia, still smiling, purse clutched before her, watched as the tall man stepped up onto the boardwalk and took her in his arms, kissing her lips.

"I knew it," Sylvia breathed, her fingers toying with Shell's shirt collar as she looked into his eyes.

"Knew what?" Shelter asked.

"Remember? I told you all I'd have to do would be to find a gathering of women to find you," Sylvia said.

"I recall." Shell picked up her suitcase and then stopped, asking her, "Say, you ain't running for anything, are you?"

"Would I get your vote?" Sylvia asked, her dark eyes bright.

"You'd better believe it." Shell's eyes swept over those fluid hips, the full breasts, the waiting, petulant mouth. "Anytime."

"Then I'm running," Sylvia said, leaning her head against Shelter Morgan's chest.

"For what?" he asked, grinning.

"For your hotel room," Sylvia answered, slipping a hand to Shelter's thigh.

"No need to run," Shelter said, picking up her suitcase again. He put his arm around her waist, and whispered into her ear, "But it wouldn't hurt to hurry a little."

FIVE FAST-ACTION NOVELS OF THE FRONTIER WEST

HOMESTEAD JUSTICE   (566, $1.95)
by Don P. Jenison
After his father was murdered by sheep herders, Greg was bent on revenge. He determined to keep his land—The Wine Cup Ranch —cow country, and he'd stop at nothing short of death to see that others observed his word.

SAGEBRUSH SHOWDOWN   (520, $1.95)
by Tom West
When Deputy Sheriff Jim Hardy finds bronkbuster Wyoming dead in an alley with a .45 slug in his back, he's faced with the blame. He sets off on a quest to find the killer, clear his own name and shoot him dead before the six-shooter shoots him.

SHELTER #1: PRISONER OF REVENGE   (598, $1.95)
by Paul Ledd
After seven years in prison for a crime he didn't commit, ex-confederate soldier, Shelter Dorsett, was free and plotting his revenge on the "friends" who had used him in their scheme and left him the blame.

GRUBSTAKE   (577, $1.95)
by E. Hoffman Price
Not even Copely and his band of roughneck crooks could stop Meander I. Gregg from staking his claim in Crater Ledge. He was strong, determined and good with a gun. No one was going to stand in his way and live to tell the tale.

FLAG   (481, $1.95)
by John Toombs
It doesn't take long for Trebor to come face-to-face with his gun-slinging past when a roughneck turns up that remembers his days as that ruthless outlaw named Slater.

Available wherever paperbacks are sold, or order direct from the Publisher. Send cover price plus 50¢ per copy for mailing and handling to Zebra Books, 21 East 40th Street, New York, N.Y. 10016. DO NOT SEND CASH!